Roy Pedersen was born in Ayrshire and brought up in Aberdeen. After a brief spell in London, where he created the first and best selling Gaelic map of Scotland, he spent most of his working life based in Inverness. There he pursued a successful career in the economic, social and cultural development of the Highlands and Islands and as a Highland councillor. He writes, publishes, speaks and broadcasts on a variety of issues connected with world affairs, and with the history, present and future development of the "New Scotland" and its wider international setting. The Odinist is his third murder mystery in the Dalmannoch series.

OTHER BOOKS BY THE SAME AUTHOR

NON-FICTION

One Europe – A Hundred Nations
Loch Ness with Jacobite – A History of Cruising on Loch Ness
Pentland Hero
George Bellairs – The Littlejohn Casebook: The 1940s
Who Pays the Ferryman?
Western Ferries – Taking on Giants
The Pedersen Chronicles
Gaelic Guerrilla (in preparation)

FICTION

Dalmannoch – The Affair of Brother Richard
Sweetheart Murder

ROY PEDERSEN

THE ODINIST

A Brother Richard Dalmannoch Mystery

First published in Scotland in 2019
Pedersen
Lochlann
8 Drummond Road
Inverness
IV2 4NA

www.pedersen.org.uk

Copyright © Roy Pedersen 2013

The moral right of Roy Pedersen to be identified as the author and illustrator of this work has been asserted by him in accordance with the Copyright, Designs and Patents Act 1988.

All rights reserved
No part of this publication may be reproduced, stored or transmitted in any form without the express written permission of the publisher.

ISBN: 978-1-912270-41-5

This book is a work of fiction. The names characters, organisations and incidents described are either imaginary or are used fictitiously and no reference is made to any living person.

British Library Cataloguing-in-Publication Data
A catalogue record for this book is available from the British Library

Printed, bound and distributed by For the Right Reasons, 38 Grant Street, Inverness, IV3 8BN

For
Wendy and Sine

CONTENTS

The Dissolute Councillor   1

The Festival   7

Hector's Woes   14

A Shipboard Encounter   21

Northwards   27

Inverness   34

Ravenblack   38

Misty Isle   44

Dalmannoch Affairs   52

Breaking News   57

Hector's Investigations   65

Ewan Allan's Movements   72

The Sabbath   79

The Presentation   86

A Close Shave   92

A Second Murder   97

Abducted   102

The Illuminati   109

Shanghaied   116

Ragnar Torkelsen's Heartbreaks   123

West across the Sea   128

Cat and Mice   134

Jimmy Ritchie   141

Iona Interlude   146

Corryvreckan   154

Sharing Stories   160

Plan of Action   166

Setting the Trap   171

Hostilities Commence   177

Interrogation   183

Sea Chase   187

To Safe Haven   194

Trouble with the Law   200

Police Deliberations and Shipboard Activities 206

Homeward Bound   212

New Love   217

Dalmannoch Developments   223

Wedding Arrangements   228

Wedding Bells   234

Epilogue   240

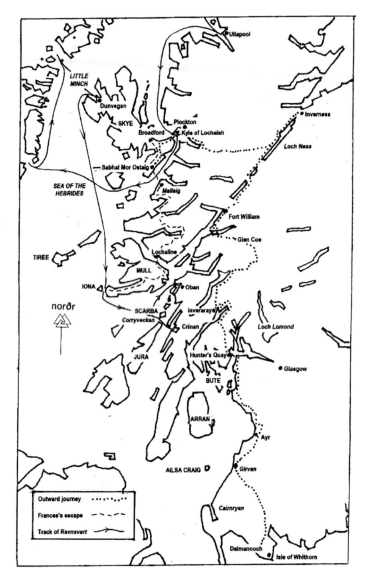

Main places mentioned and showing the journeys of Richard and Frances

THE DISSOLUTE COUNCILLOR

A SLEEK BLACK HULLED MOTOR YACHT headed purposely southwards through the Sound of Sleat, the waterway that divides the Inner Hebridean Island of Skye from the Scottish mainland.

Viewing the yacht's progress from Camas Cross on the Skye shore, it was Kirsty Anna Mackinnon who first saw the body floating at the water's edge. At first she thought it was a seal. Then the realization dawned that this was no seal. She grabbed her boyfriend's arm.

"Oh my God Iain! Look!"

Iain Campbell followed her gaze and saw, partly covered in seaweed, the half-submerged figure of a man, face down, slowly bobbing in the tide-line wavelets caused by the passing vessel's wash. Iain inspected the figure. It was that of a middle aged man dressed in a dark business suit. He pulled the body a little up the beach. There was no sign of life

"We'll need to get help. Kirsty. Go up to the house there and call the police. I'll stay here on guard."

Half an hour later the police were at the scene. The young lovers were briefly questioned and then dismissed. The body was later identified as that of Ewan Allan MacLeod, an elected member of the Highland Council.

* * *

Councillor MacLeod had not come home on the two previous nights. He ran a guest house near Broadford with his wife Shona. In truth, it was Shona who ran the business, for Councillor MacLeod was often away in

Inverness at Council meetings or locally at the Masonic lodge or who knew where. He had his strengths as a councillor; affable, a persuasive orator and ready to support those in need. Of late too he had also been active and 'away' on some 'hush-hush' inter-authority group looking at the merits or otherwise of greater political autonomy for the Scottish islands. On the other hand, as a man, everyone knew that he drank too much and when in his cups he could be nasty, aggressive and vindictive. It was quite well known too that he had a fancy woman in Inverness.

Mrs MacLeod was well used to her husband's absences. Inverness was two hour's drive away – two and a half, if the traffic was bad. When there was a morning council meeting, it was quite usual for Ewan to drive over the night before, or to stay on if he was already there. What irritated her was when he 'forgot' to tell her. It was not so much that she missed him, but that the uncertainty spoilt her own plans. Normally he would ring the following day to explain that a special evening meeting had been called, or he had bumped into an acquaintance, had gone for a dram and daren't drive, or some such.

On this occasion, after a second night without any contact, she had phoned the Council HQ. He had not been seen there that week. She tried the lodge. Again there had been no sign of him there. So they said, although she suspected the brethren sometimes covered up for him if he had been on the 'ran-dan'.

At midday she rang the local police to let them know that she was becoming concerned. She was reassured that they would put the word out and let her know as soon as they found out where he was. As a public

2

figure Councillor MacLeod was of course well known to the police.

For the rest of the day she busied herself with the duties that befall a guest house proprietrix. As she did so she thought about her lot. They had not been blessed with children, but they were comfortable enough financially. When they were young, Ewan had been good-looking, witty and as elder brother stood to inherit the croft on which the guest house now stood. When Ewan's parents had assigned the croft to them, the young couple, with a generous grant from the then Highland Board, built the guest house alongside the old croft house. The latter remained the home of Ewan's parents until they passed away. It was now a self-catering holiday cottage producing a useful income. Yes they were comfortable enough, and she enjoyed the status of going to civic functions as a councillor's wife. It was just that Ewan had gone to seed and they had grown apart.

She thought of Ewan's younger brother, Donald Angus, a different kettle of fish. As a young man he had been in Ewan's shadow with, it seemed, lesser prospects. He went to sea, saw the world and eventually gained his mate's ticket. Then he got the call to the ministry and was ordained as the Reverend Donald Angus MacLeod with a church way down in the rural far south west of Scotland. He had married Jessie, a happy-go-lucky farmer's daughter and now they had five lively children.

From what she had heard, while by no means well off, they had a happy and fulfilling life. Donald Angus was far removed from the oft-caricatured straight-laced, sanctimonious West Highland preacher. Larger than life, he was an accomplished piper and leader of a group of Gaelic learners based at some sort of cultural centre called

3

Dalmannoch. He seemed to have struck up a rapport with the manager there, a former Catholic monk called Brother Richard.

A television programme on BBC Alba the week before had featured Dalmannoch as the venue of a music festival that seemed to have attracted a large, weird and wonderful collection of folkies, New Agers, Pagans, Christians and not a few 'normal' individuals. And there on screen was the burly and bearded Donald with dog collar and pipes under his arm extoling, in his fluent native Gaelic, Dalmannoch's creed of sectarian tolerance. To Shona, it seemed like another world.

These thoughts were banished by the arrival of a couple of Germans on tour by motor cycle. They had been booked in by the tourist information centre. These were followed in due course by the usual mix of visitors – English, Dutch, Japanese plus the two electricians from Glasgow, booked in for a few days to upgrade a local sub-station. Each was shown their quarters. There was the meal to prepare and serve and advice to be given as to local events, beauty spots and sites of interest, of which there are many on Skye.

Late that evening two uniformed police officers, a male and female, rang the front door bell. Shona MacLeod opened the door and could tell immediately by the grave expression on the officers' faces that something serious was afoot.

"Mrs MacLeod, I'm afraid I have some very bad news."

"Come in. Please come in."

She showed the two officers into the dining room, for there were still guests in the lounge.

"Mrs MacLeod, I'm Sergeant Steven Nicolson and this is WPC Gillies. I think it would be best if you sat down,"

She did so.

"I'm afraid your husband's body was found earlier today in the sea, by the shore at Camas Cross."

Shona MacLeod said nothing. She was stunned.

The police woman put her hand on Shona's.

"I'm sorry."

For a time Shona was silent.

"What happened? Why . . . ? Oh God!"

The officers allowed time for the awful truth to sink in and then the police-woman spoke again.

"Councillor MacLeod's body has been taken to Inverness for *post mortem*. We need you to come to identify the body. If you would be so kind."

"What tonight? *Mo chreach* ! I have guests in the house. I've . . ."

"No, no not tonight. Of course not. We can take you tomorrow by police car."

And so it was that Shona MacLeod arranged for her neighbour, Hettie Henderson, to cover for her in the guest house and set off with heavy heart after breakfast the following morning for Raigmore Hospital in Inverness. She drove her own car rather than be stuck in the company of the police for a whole day.

She presented herself at reception as arranged and was accompanied to the morgue by an Inspector MacGillivray for the harrowing process of identification. There was no doubt. It *was* Ewan. The inspector then asked her to follow him by car to the Burnett Road Police Station. The shock of confirmation of her husband's

5

identity was compounded by the inspector's surprise revelation.

"Mrs MacLeod, I'm afraid I have to tell you that a *post mortem* has been carried out on Councillor MacLeod and it seems that the cause of death is strangulation and that this happened before his immersion in the sea. We are treating this as a case of murder."

THE FESTIVAL

DALMANNOCH'S first music festival had been a greater success than any dared hope. The key to this success had been the agreement by the celebrated bandana wearing folk singer, Donnelly Dolan, to be headline act, and to waive his fee. The 'Twittersphere' had buzzed wildly and, after a wet and windy spell, the favourable weather forecast for that September weekend had been vindicated by a glorious Indian summer. Such was this combination that the attendees numbered thousands rather than the hundreds anticipated.

Donnelly Dolan, born and raised in Cumbernauld, had moved to London to make his name while still in his teens. For some years it had been a struggle on the breadline, running the circuit of clubs and pubs, learning his trade the hard way. It is one of those odd quirks of the music industry, however, that it was in Germany and Scandinavia that he first achieved a measure of recognition and financial success, after which he built up a substantial fan base within the British folk scene. Then Dolan's recent tour of America shot his "Moonshine Girl" to near the top of the US charts, making him a pile of money. That the Dalmannoch crew had been able to attract such a megastar as Donnelly Dolan was a cause for amazement and not a little jealousy among other entertainment promoters.

There were several other acts of mixed, but in the main, reasonable quality. "Irrepressible" Barney Brown and his Bluegrass Bunch who, on stage, sounded as though they had materialized from deepest Kentucky, but hailed in fact from Dalkeith on the outskirts of Edinburgh,

as evidenced by their off stage Midlothian accents.
Among the acts from further afield were sing-along
Dickie Byrd and the Twitters from Somerset and, as part
of her European tour, the haunting lyrics of Texan, Sadie
Sim. Local acts featured too. Six members of
Dalmannoch's own Galloway Gaelic Group had formed a
singing sextet, led by Agnes Morrison, one of the group's
tutors. Their catchy Gaelic songs found an appreciative
audience, an impact somewhat overwhelmed by the skirl
of the Reverend Donald Angus MacLeod's pipe tunes that
got the whole assembly up and dancing.

To quote Duggie Gordon, Chartered Accountant
and one of the original prime-movers of the Galloway
Gaelic Group, Donald Angus was, "very broad minded
for a minister."

Truly, the rugged reverend gentleman from the
Isle of Skye was in many respects the life and soul of the
event. He acted as joint festival compare, alongside the
well-known Edinburgh comedian, Ronnie Hall. The
upbeat efforts of this pair maintained a breathless pace.

Of course the success of any festival is due as
much to preparation, promotion and management as to the
quality of the performances on stage. This was no less
true of Dalmannoch's Music Festival. The behind-the-
scenes team was controlled by the Dalmannoch Trust
which, since the year before, had owned and managed the
buildings and land of Dalmannoch as a cultural centre in
the rural heart of the Galloway Machars.

Day to day management is in the hands of ex-
monk Brother Richard Wells and his lover, ex-nursing
sister Frances McGarrigle. How this unlikely pairing
came together to renovate the near derelict Dalmannoch

into a functioning cultural centre is a long story[1], but suffice it to say that they are supported by an effective board of trustees and an enthusiastic band of supporters and associates.

Prominent among the trustees are wealthy Canadian benefactor Hector Woodrow Douglas and Professor Ruairidh Alasdair Macdonald, Head of the Inverness based MacPhedran Institute of Celtic Studies, of which Dalmannoch is its southern outpost. The institute had recently taken on a new part-time research fellow, Angela Trevelyan, who had taken on the task of studying the history of the Order of the Galloway Knights of Peace, otherwise known as the Elven Knights – a shadowy group of medieval origin.

Another trustee, motherly Holly Garden is the priestess of the neo-Pagan Wigtown Wicca Coven which periodically uses the small, but curiously decorated, Dalmannoch chapel for its sabbats – such is the sectarian breadth and tolerance of this unusual centre.

It was the ideas and inspiration of another coven member, the talented and stunningly beautiful blond haired Suzie Silver that had much to do with the success of the festival. She had first suggested Donnelly Dolan as headline act and she, through the Wiccan network, had secured his services, for, although he does not broadcast the fact, Dolan is himself a practicing Pagan.

As befitted his superstar status, the trust had been able to buy, second-hand and for a knock-down price (it being the end of the season) a residential caravan. This

---

[1] For the full background see "Dalmannoch – The Affair of Brother Richard", ISBN: 978-1-9057787-68-5 and "Sweetheart Murder", ISBN: 978-1-905787-93-7.

large trailer was transported to site a week before the commencement of the festival, spruced up, and for the duration of the festival was abode to Dolan and his roadie Whisky (real name John Walker).

The folk singer relied on Whisky as driver, sound engineer, travel agent and general factotum. Like Dolan, Whisky was a Pagan, not, however, of the Wiccan persuasion but of the Old Norse Viking form of Paganism which he had absorbed whilst on tour in Scandinavia. In demonstration of his orientation, Whisky wore a silver Thor's hammer on a leather thong round his neck. A lean 29 year old, with moustache, pony tail and a dry wit, he needed a sense of humour to cope with Dolan's temperamental outbursts. These tantrums notwithstanding, the two had a way of going that was part of the secret of the last hectic year's success.

Conscious of signs of burn-out, Dolan confided to Whisky:

"Hey man, Dalmannoch's my last public gig for now. I'm knackered. I need to cool it – work up new lyrics – take a break. "

Whisky would remain on the payroll but his services would not be required for a couple of months.

When the festival was over, he felt he deserved release from work. Whisky drove Dolan home to *Avalon*, his recently purchased Borders pad, but elected the following day to return to the Dalmannoch caravan.

It may be wondered what motivated this move. The reason, and an unexpected one, was that during the festival, Whisky had struck up a rapport with Holly Garden, each curious, but tolerant of the other's spiritual path. The plumpish Holly was twenty years older than Whisky, but the two seemed to hit it off. On Whisky's return the liaison developed into a torrid, if improbable, love affair. Gone were Holly's long skirts, wraps and unstyled long greying hair; their place taken by a short black skirt, low-cut scarlet blouse and 'big' blond tinted hair. The transformation was astonishing.

* * *

A successful conclusion to the festival was a matter of great importance for the Dalmannoch crew. What had sparked off the idea of mounting a festival in the first place was the realization that the Dalmannoch enterprise in its existing form was not sustainable. It needed to generate new sources of income. To this end, plans to develop Dalmannoch as a venue for weddings, conferences, residential courses and the like, could not be realized properly unless increased accommodation could be created and that required significant finance. This, the trustees lacked, and so the festival had been seen as the best means of kick-starting a fund. One small but important alteration that was carried out on the building was removing the partition wall between reception and dining room to create a bigger general purpose gathering and catering area.

Post festival, once the dust had settled, the litter had been cleared and financial outcome assessed, those trustees who were to hand, plus a few associates, met in Dalmannoch's library. Duggie Gordon, who, besides his involvement with the Gaelic Group, is the foundation's somewhat pedantic secretary and treasurer. He was able to announce:

"Ehem – well now – Let me see."

He shuffled through his printed spread sheets and hand-written notes.

"I haven't been able to undertake a complete analysis of the festival account, but I have, on the one hand, summated the expenditure in terms of hire of marquee, stage, equipment, fees, licence, police and security costs, advertising and other sundry items. I have set this, on the other hand, against box office revenue, concession fees, merchandising and other income. I am – ehem – able to say that – subject to clarification of some outstanding items – we have made a net profit, in round figures, of £45,000."

There were whoops of delight and mutual hugs.

When the hubbub subsided, it was Brother Richard who took the floor.

"Well friends; that is a better outcome than I think any of us dared hope. You are all to be congratulated on the huge effort you have put in. Without the good weather and Donnelley Dolan's generous agreement to head the line-up, things could have been very different. A special thank you to you Suzie for fixing that – Dolan I mean, not the weather. I don't think even your impressive powers can influence meteorological conditions – but then again . . ."

He then made reference to absent trustees who would have to be informed of this welcome financial outcome. Hector Woodrow Douglas was in Canada pursuing some urgent business matters and Professor Macdonald involved in beginning of term activity in Inverness.

Brother Richard continued:

"This is the first step in assembling the funding for the building work which we hope will give Dalmannoch the critical mass to secure a sustainable future. In a way, the mobile home we acquired for accommodating Donnelly Dolan and John Walker, or should I say Whisky, is already the first modest, if perhaps temporary, step in extending our sleeping accommodation."

Richard then went over to Frances, took her hand and she rose to stand beside him.

"With regard to expanded activity for our centre, I have something of a personal announcement to make. As you all know Frances and I have been together for over a year and we are now blessed with the prospect of a child."

More cheers and clapping.

"Coming from a former monk, my next announcement is perhaps a little tardy, but Frances and I plan to marry in Dalmannoch's wonderful Chapel. Father McGuire has agreed to carry out the sacrament."

There was another round of cheers and congratulatory hugs.

The ex-monk let the excitement die down.

"Before we tie the knot, however, we are shortly heading off for a couple of weeks for a tour of the Highlands and Islands."

HECTOR'S WOES

FIVE thousand miles away on Canada's Pacific coast, the Dalmannoch Foundation's most generous benefactor, Hector Woodrow Douglas, had been facing serious problems. As president of Woodrow Douglas Logistics, he was fighting for the company's very survival.

Over the previous quarter of a century, taking advantage of the opening up of trade with China, Hector had grown his freight forwarding enterprise from small beginnings into a significant international operation with Vancouver as its hub. The business had reached the point at which Hector had begun to take a back seat and to leave the day to day management to his son James. James, as holder of twenty five percent of the equity, had proven to be an able and hard-working managing director.

Hector's beautiful, but empty-headed daughter, Elaine, as a non-executive director with ten percent, had little real understanding of, or interest in, the complexities of the logistics business. She relied on her Californian banker husband, Brad, to advise her prior to board meetings. Hector had never really taken to Brad Linley. Brad was manager of the Vancouver Branch of Western Universal Bank.

James's wife Lynda, was different; intelligent, a partner in a prestigious accountancy firm, mother of two boys and supportive of her husband. Almost too good to be true, Hector sometimes felt.

One of the two non-family directors was Pricilla Munro, a partner in one of Vancouver's well regarded accountancy firms. She acted as Woodrow Douglas Logistics' Finance Director with a five percent stake. Her seriousness and precision of thought contrasted with Elaine's lack thereof. In fact she found it difficult to hide her disdain for Elaine.

Things had been fine with Woodrow Douglas Logistics until a bid had been made by Whiteman Inc, a large American corporation, to buy out Woodrow Douglas Logistics. Although Elaine, on the urging of Brad, had been keen to sell, Hector had no wish to see his hard earned life's work and his family's inheritance sold off, particularly while the company had much potential for growth. The bid was turned down flat.

Within a month, contracts were mysteriously cancelled, spurious orders never materialized and containers were misdirected. Where formerly labour relations had been harmonious, a strike was now threatened. It wasn't long before these events started to have an effect on both income, and worse, the firm's reputation.

What was causing this extraordinary deterioration in what had, up until the takeover bid, been a smooth-running operation? A special board meeting was called. Hector sensed conspiracy:

"These incidents are no coincidence. There's some hidden hand at work. It's got to be sabotage and it's all happened since we turned down the Whiteman bid. The thing is how do we combat it?"

Apart from Elaine, who suggested that Hector was becoming paranoid, there was agreement that dirty tricks were in play. What was not clear was how to combat this threat to the business.

From time to time, Woodrow Douglas Logistics had engaged a specialist firm of corporate lawyers to handle delicate legal matters. The firm's representative was Eustace Blake, a small dapper man of somewhat enigmatic demeanor. He had a reputation as a clever fixer of knotty legal problems which resulted in him travelling widely to satisfy the needs of his international clientele. Eustace was unmarried. The love of his life was his small yacht *Mary Jane* (his late mother's name) in which, in such limited spare time as he had, he explored the Gulf Islands and the creeks and inlets of the Puget Sound – gunk-holing, as he described it. Blake had recently been made a director of Woodrow Douglas Logistics with a five percent share, the second non-family stockholder. He was persuaded to agree with Hector that something irregular was afoot.

The first clue came from Hector's old friend and faithful business associate, Chang Wu. Chang, who ran a substantial import-export operation, was based in Hong Kong, with offices also in Shanghai and Guangzhou. He phoned Hector, puzzled as to why a substantial shipment he had placed with Woodrow Douglas had been diverted to another agency – none other than Whiteman.

Outraged at this blatant subversion of his business, Hector enlisted Chang's help and with a little discreet digging, Chang supplied as much detail of the electronic paper trail at his end as he could. With this information, and not trusting anyone else, Hector and James initiated an internal investigation of the company's transactions. Much of this was carried out at night when the office was quiet.

James brought in his friend Cy Bennett, a genius at forensic information technology analysis. James and Cy had been at McGill University together and shared an interest in jazz. Besides his computer skills, Cy was a virtuoso on the sax. James, while no virtuoso on the clarinet, enjoyed nothing better than a jam session with Cy and a few other close jazz buddies.

There was no time for jazz during the investigation.

It was not long before a series of irregular but well-disguised transactions seemed to point to one individual – a recently appointed senior shipping clerk Luigi Cassani.

Cassani had a reputation for hard work. He often worked late. James and Cy waited until the senior clerk had left the building and the office was otherwise deserted. Once in his room, Cy switched on Cassani's computer. At first it seemed as though things were normal, then Cy found, how, using a duplicate domain, the clerk had fraudulently told Chang and others that shipments they had consigned via Woodrow Douglas had been over-booked, but that alternative arrangements could be made via Whiteman Inc.

As Cy and James dug deeper, they were astonished by the sheer quantity of such deliberate re-direction of traffic away from his employer. At this rate the company would be bust within a couple of months.

James opened Cassani's desk drawers – routine directories, company manuals and the like, and then a draft letter to the Vancouver Chapter of the Longshore Workers' Union suggesting that Woodrow Douglas Logistics was undermining wage and conditions agreements. One other single sheet of paper was headed by an illustration of a small stylized pyramid, underscored, in small capital letters, by the word 'ILLUMINATI'.

The paper carried the simple legend:

Succeed and you will be rewarded
You know the price of failure

"Well Cy. Thanks to you, it looks as though we've found the source of the company's recent troubles. Wait till I tell the old man."

Cy printed out examples of the incriminating emails and way-bills. With these and other documentation, James headed for Hector's house. It was well after midnight when a yawning pyjama-clad Hector opened the front door to find his son eager for an audience.

"Pop, I think we've cracked it. Have a look at this."

James described the night's investigation and its findings. Hector examined the documentation, then for a time sat in silence absorbing the significance of Cy's and James's researches. He contemplated his next move.

"Son, you and Cy've done good work this night. I reckon you may well have saved the business. I think that deserves a dram."

He rummaged in a cocktail cabinet and extracted a bottle of 18 year old Glenlivet malt whisky. He poured a measure into each of two cut crystal glasses and added a little water. He passed one glass to James. They raised their respective drinks.

"Slàinte Mhath"
"Slàinte Mhath"[2]

They each savoured the choice Speyside malt and then Hector chivvied:

---

[2] Gaelic for Good health, pronounced <u>Slan</u> tshi <u>vah</u>

"We have to be up early tomorrow." Looking at the mantle clock, he corrected himself; "I mean this morning. You stay here tonight and let's get a couple of hour's shut-eye. Then we'll nail this bastard Cassani."

By six thirty, father and son were already in the office. Hector had not slept well. He had been mulling over the previous evening's revelations.

"You've exposed Cassani, but there's got to be somebody bigger behind this – and I bet the finger points to Whiteman Inc."

Hector sat behind Cassani's desk and switched on the computer. James sat to one side on a guest chair awaiting events.

At ten past eight Luigi Cassani opened his office door. He gasped as he found the company president and managing director occupying his domain.

"Good morning Luigi. Come in. Come in and see what we've found."

Cassani made a nervous effort to bluff –

"G – good morning, eh – what can I – em . . ?"

Hector spread the incriminating print-outs on the desk. His voice was quiet and calm. He raised his eyebrow.

"Interesting, aren't they? – mmm? Re-directing our business to Whiteman Inc."

Hector waited.

Cassani, red faced, spluttered:

"I – I – I thought . . ."

"You thought you'd ruin this business that I have spent my working life building up. You thought you'd bring this company down. You piece of shit. Why? Mmm?"

19

"I – I – I didn't mean . . I had to . . . No I – I – I can't say. I . . ."

"Look Cassani. You're finished. I hope you don't suffer from claustrophobia, because you're going to spend a long time in the poky. You know what? They may go easy on you if you tell me who put you up to this."

"No one. No one – No I can't – I needed – I . . ."

At that he fell into a sullen silence, all colour drained from his face.

Luigi Cassani was escorted from the premises.

* * *

On further investigation over the next two days, the full extent of Cassani's fraud was uncovered. Clients were contacted to have recent events explained and to be reassured that henceforth business would return to normal.

The circumstances of Cassani's appointment were examined. He had apparently come with an impeccable resumé, which on investigation proved to have been fabricated. It also transpired that one of his referees had been an executive with the Western Universal Bank, the same bank that employed Brad Linley.

Cassani was released on bail, paid by a law firm on behalf of an un-named source. Within a week of his release, his body was dragged from the waters of Vancouver's False Creek.

A SHIPBOARD ENCOUNTER

J UST after breakfast, Richard and Frances headed off in Frances' yellow Renault Megane on the first proper holiday the pair had had together since they had set up home in Dalmannoch over a year before. The mood was one of excited anticipation.

After consulting the map and considering options, they had decided, on the advice of "The Rev", to take a westerly route.

As they drove north past Newton Stewart on the A714, Frances took first turn at the wheel. She had been suffering bouts of morning sickness until a couple of days before, but now she felt good and ready for the journey ahead:

"I can't wait to see the real Highlands and Islands. We've heard so much from Donald and Agnes and from Professor Ruairidh too, that it seems as though we already know the place, yet we have never been. I hope it lives up to expectations."

Richard, with the road atlas on his lap, was in full agreement whilst admiring the passing scene as the car left Galloway behind and entered the ancient province of Carrick,

"In a way, it's a whole new adventure, but let's hope a bit more relaxing than the last few months."

In fact, apart from the hectic preparations for the music festival and the running of the event itself, earlier that summer they had gone through the traumatic aftermath of the murder of their colleague Colin McCulloch. In dealing with this issue Richard and their

Pagan friend Thomas Nutter had been lucky to escape with their lives[3].

"Too right," Frances concurred, "A relaxing adventure, No more fighting the forces of darkness."

"Agreed?"

"Agreed."

They drove on down into Girvan from which the great volcanic plug that forms the now uninhabited island of Ailsa Craig dominated the seaward horizon. The Renault sped northwards past Ayr and on to the dual carriageway which took them just past Ardrossan, with Arran's majestic mountains now filling the seaward view.

And on up the scenic Clyde Coast, past Seamill, Fairlie, Largs, Wemyss Bay and the Cloch, with respectively the islands of the Wee and Great Cumbraes and Bute and then the Cowal peninsula to seaward, until the ferry terminal at McInroy's Point was reached. There, Frances turned the car left, to join the queue for the ferry across to Cowal and the forthcoming journey through Argyll.

They waited for the next ferry, but they didn't have to wait long for the service is frequent. The bright red *Sound of Shuna* arrived, locked on to the link-span and disgorged its incoming load of vehicles and foot passengers. The Renault then joined the convoy of vehicles rolling aboard. Once parked on the vehicle deck, a sailor collected the fare and issued a ticket. The pair then made their way to the open deck above the passenger saloon to observe the vessel's departure.

---

[3] For the full story see "Sweetheart Murder", ISBN: 978-1-905787-93-7.

A few minutes later and they were off on the twenty minute passage. They admired the dramatic unfolding panorama. To the south the Firth of Clyde opened up, framed by the now distant Arran mountains. Ahead, westwards, the Cowal shore and the Holy Loch beckoned, while northwards brooding mountains embraced the fjord-like Loch Long.

A fellow passenger, sensing that Richard and Frances were first time travellers on the route, struck up conversation.

"Look there's a nuclear submarine from Faslane heading to sea."

They followed his finger to discern a low dark shape emerging from the upper firth and turning through the ferry's wake onto a southerly course.

Richard took in this sinister vessel's progress and felt urged to comment.

"Wouldn't it be a better world if we didn't have to have these fearful weapons threatening death and destruction?"

The other responded:

"It would. And the sooner they are removed from Scotland the better. I wonder what fool thought it a good idea to locate a nuclear target not twenty miles from Scotland's biggest city.

I'm Angus MacPhedran, by the way. I'm one of the local councillors. You're both on holiday I presume."

On confirming that they were, and introducing themselves, Richard explained that they were based at Dalmannoch in Galloway.

"Ah yes, I've heard of Dalmannoch. Wasn't there a music festival there last week? I saw something about it on the telly. I'm on the council's Events and Festivals Committee myself. How did it all go?"

After a brief description of the successful outcome of the Dalmannoch event, Frances remarked on the councillor's name:

"MacPhedran? An unusual name. The only time I heard it before is the name of an organization in Inverness – the MacPhedran Institute of Celtic Studies. It's headed up by a friend of ours, Professor Ruairidh Macdonald. You may have heard of him. In fact we're going to stay with him and his family tonight, as part of our tour, before we head off to the Isle of Skye and a weekend Gaelic course at the college there."

"Well well well. Yes indeed, I have met Professor Macdonald and a very erudite man he is. And I can tell you that it was my great great uncle Aneas MacPhedran who set up the institute in the nineteen twenties. He was a noted Gaelic scholar, which sadly I am not. Small world though, isn't it. In fact for all its size, Highland Scotland is a big village really. You can't stay invisible for long – even if you want to."

By this point in the conversation, the *Sound of Shuna* was approaching the Cowal terminal at Hunter's Quay and the ship's public address system instructed passengers to return to their cars to prepare for disembarkation. Before doing so, Councillor MacPhedran, who had taken rather a shine to Richard and Frances, suggested a bite of lunch at the nearby Royal Marine Hotel before they went their separate ways.

Over lunch they exchanged potted life-stories. Councillor MacPhedran then suggested some places worth visiting in Argyll, included in which were a number of the southern Inner Hebridean islands. He added:

"Talking of islands, I'm just on my way back from a meeting last night in Edinburgh with the Scottish Government and councillors from island authorities. There's a movement, you see, to press for greater autonomy for the islands – more control over resources such as the sea-bed and energy, tourism and such like. It was quite a difficult meeting."

Richard asked, "I suppose the government wasn't keen to let go of its powers."

"No, no it wasn't that. The Government reps were actually quite open to consider the issue. No there was dissent among the council representatives. You see, our authority and the Highland Council have been side-lined, because although between us we include many islands, we also have substantial mainland territories. On top of that, with power comes responsibility and this is where the problem lies. I suppose I shouldn't say too much, but there was a real bust-up between the man from the Highland Council and the woman from Shetland. The Highland man – Councillor Ewan Allan MacLeod from Skye was so irate that he thumped the table and stormed out of the meeting. Betty Anderson, the official from Shetland, was reduced to tears."

"How embarrassing for all concerned. What caused this outburst?" Richard asked.

"Well in a way, it was a storm in a tea-cup – you might say an unwarranted cultural clash. You see Shetlanders are proud of their Norse heritage, while Councillor MacLeod has always been a strong supporter of the Gaelic language and culture. In the course of the discussion, Betty Anderson mentioned that different American and Norwegian groups were showing an interest in the affairs of the Scottish islands and their potential for renewable energy. It was this that led to Councillor MacLeod's outburst:

'Yanks?! Muscling in where they're not wanted. And bloody meddling Vikings! We threw *them* out of the Hebrides seven hundred years ago. They'll make a comeback over my dead body!'

The irony is that his own surname, MacLeod is partially Norse: Gaelic *Mac* and Norse *Ljot*."

NORTHWARDS

AFTER lunch, Councillor MacPhedran took his leave of the holidaymakers to head for an Events and Festivals meeting in Dunoon. Richard and Frances set off north westwards along the shore of the Holy Loch and then Loch Eck and through Glenbranter to reach the eastern shore of Loch Fyne at Strachur.

Admiring the rugged scenery as they went, Richard was mulling over what Councillor MacPhedran had told them about himself, places to see and about the meeting in Edinburgh.

"Odd, isn't it the business of that Councillor MacLeod storming out of that meeting the way he did. It seems so trivial. I wonder why he has such a downer on Norwegians."

"And Americans," added Frances.

As they continued northward and round the head of Loch Fyne, talking of this and that, Frances returned to the topic.

"MacLeod – MacLeod – I was just having a wee think; didn't our own Rev Donald Angus say he had a brother in Skye who was a councillor. I wonder if he's the same man."

"Mm – intriguing – could be. If so, he sounds to be a very different sort of character from our Donald. Perhaps we'll find out more when we get to Skye."

By three o'clock they had reached Inveraray. After a quick look round this attractive planned town, they headed for Inveraray Castle, the ancestral seat of the Dukes of Argyll, chiefs of the once powerful Clan Campbell. While Richard was somewhat ambivalent about displays of aristocratic wealth and privilege,

Frances had a sneaking fascination for landed proprietors and their country houses. So they paid their £9 entrance fees and after passing through the modest entrance hall, were duly impressed by the grandeur of the state rooms, the displays of weaponry, the opulence of the décor, the paintings and the centuries of history.

After three quarters of an hour or so, it was time to leave and continue the journey. Richard remarked as they made their way back to the car:

"The Campbells certainly seem to have been pretty adept at choosing the winning side as they advanced their power. Do you remember Ruairidh (Professor MacDonald) saying – 'The Campbells were aye fishing in drumlie waters.' Mind you, as a MacDonald, I suppose he would say that."

In defence of the Campbells Frances retorted:

"Well sure they certainly built a beautiful castle."

. Once on the road again, with Richard at the wheel now, the Renault headed up Glen Aray, to the north end of Loch Awe, making a right turn onto the A 85 for some twelve miles eastwards to Tyndrum. On this section the road runs parallel to the Oban railway so that a Glasgow bound train paced the car for several miles. A right turn at Tyndrum and the route took a northerly course past Bridge of Orchy and on to the great high plateau of Rannoch Moor. Frances was mesmerized:

"What scenery we have been through today, sea, islands, lochs, mountains, forests and now this, heather moor, lochans and wee islands all mixed together almost as far as the eye can see. It's an amazing country."

As they progressed, steep rocky mountains closed in on the road. The Renault started its winding descent into deep Glen Coe.

"Och, look at that. Wisps of mist on the mountains, the rocks, the shadows, cascades of water; it's like a scene from some epic drama."

Richard agreed and pointed out that indeed over three hundred years before a most treacherous deed was enacted.

"It was Ruairidh, who first told me. He's steeped in Clan Donald lore. Then I read about it in a book by a man called Prebble. It all stemmed from the demand by King William of Orange for the Highland chiefs to sign an oath of allegiance following the defeat of the first Jacobite Rising. Alastair MacIain, 12th Chief of the MacDonalds of Glencoe, was late in signing partly because of winter snow. However, the Lord Advocate John Dalrymple, the Master of Stair, hated the Highlanders and their Gaelic way of life. He had actually hoped that the Jacobite chiefs would have declined the oath, so as to give him the chance to break the clan system. MacIain's certificate was deemed to be irregular and the Master of Stair persuaded the King to sign an order to 'extirpate' the MacDonalds of Glencoe.

John Campbell, a senior member of the Campbell clan, saw an opportunity for revenge against past grievances. A company of Campbell Government troops was billeted on the MacDonalds in Glencoe. MacIain received them in the hospitable tradition of the Highlands. In the early morning the Campbell troops set upon the unsuspecting MacDonalds. 38 men, including MacIain himself, were murdered either in their homes or as they tried to flee the glen. Another 40 defenseless women and children died of exposure in the February snow after their homes were burned. This infamous atrocity became known as the Massacre of Glencoe and I suppose accounts for the ill feeling between Ruairidh and Campbells generally."

Frances was shaken by this story.

"How awful for those poor people. I'm glad we live in more civilized times."

"Me too, but then look at parts of the world today. This sort of thing is still going on."

For a time a sense of gloom pervaded the car, but this lightened as the shore of Loch Leven was reached, after which they passed through the former slate quarrying village of Ballachulish and then over the Ballachulish Bridge to reach Fort William, where a stop was made for toilets, a stretch of the legs and something to eat.

Their hasty repast was haddock and chips, eaten *al fresco* by the side of Loch Linnhe. As they sat on a bench by the waterfront, a smallish white working ship caught Richard's eye as she made her way seawards down the loch. He went back to the car to retrieve the binoculars and focused on the passing vessel.

"Mm, unusual little ship. Some kind of work ship or survey vessel by the look of her. I can just make out the name *Whiteman Pioneer*. I wonder where she's heading."

Time was pressing, however, and Frances was anxious to progress as far as possible before darkness set in. The pair set off again up the Great Glen past Loch Lochy, Loch Oich and by the time Fort Augustus was reached, it was dark. Following instructions, which Frances had noted down, they proceeded for the last twenty or so miles and finally up a side road until they reached *A Cheapach*, the house of their good friend Professor Ruairidh Alasdair Macdonald.

Even before they had alighted from the car, a somewhat tired looking Ruairidh had opened his front door and was striding towards the car.

"Oh, you two are a sight for sore eyes, after what I've been through over the last few days. But come in and welcome to my humble abode."

He gave Frances a warm hug and a kiss and put his arm round Richard's shoulder and ushered them both inside his, in fact, far from humble dwelling.

"I'll get your bags in a minute. First let me show you the layout of the place. It's a pity it's dark, because the view from here over loch Ness is pretty stunning."

The house had originally been a modest two up and two down dormer windowed cottage that had been added to at various times, such that it now sprawled to about three times its original size on about an acre of land. The interior was comfortable and in good taste with large lounge, dining room, library, kitchen, toilet and utility room on the ground floor. Upstairs, bedrooms and bathrooms were connected on slightly varying levels via rambling passages. Throughout the house the walls displayed a goodly collection of paintings and other art-works.

Once settled and freshened up in the generous double guest bedroom, Richard and Frances returned to the lounge and to Ruairidh. Frances looked round expectantly:

"Where are Fiona and the girls now? Are they out? I'm so looking forward to meeting them."

Ruairidh paused. He cast his eyes down.

"Well, I'm afraid I have bad news. Fiona has left and she's taken the girls with her. She's gone off with a

31

musician, and to make matters worse he's a Campbell! His name's Dale Campbell."

Frances was stunned at Ruairidh's news. Although Richard and she had never actually met Ruairidh's wife Fiona or his twin daughters Catriona and Eilidh, they had always been under the impression that the marriage had been a happy and stable one.

"Oh Ruairidh! What on earth happened?"

"Well, I suppose it's partly my fault. I've been away a lot at Dalmannoch and elsewhere over the past year. She just upped and left with the girls last week. I'm devastated."

Frances sympathized.

"I'm so sorry, Ruairidh."

Ruairidh continued:

"The thing is, Fiona's on the committee of the Dualchas[4] Festival. It's a kind of Highlands and Islands wide programme of music events. The committee chairman is a Councillor Ewan Allan MacLeod. He's a bit of a dodgy character by all accounts, but pretty effective in promoting Highland culture. Anyway, it seems Councillor MacLeod brought in Dale Campbell because of his celebrity as a musician and his industry connections. That's how Fiona and Campbell met. I hate to admit it, but, compared with boring old me, he's good looking, amusing and talented."

Frances put her arm round Ruairidh.

---

[4] Gaelic meaning heritage, tradition: pronounced <u>Dooal</u> chass ("ch" as in Scottish loch)

"Och Ruairidh, you're far from boring. You're a highly talented and much loved man – and a very attractive one."

Ruairidh forced a weak smile.

INVERNESS

AT breakfast the following morning Professor Ruairidh Alasdair Macdonald seemed to be in a cheerier frame of mind. The conversation at table ranged over topics unconnected with the academic's domestic problems.

"I'm afraid I'll have to go into work shortly. Why don't you follow me in half an hour or so and I'll show you round the office? And then you can explore Inverness."

And so, following Ruairidh's directions, with Richard at the wheel, the Renault Megane headed for Inverness. After parking the car in the Eastgate multi-storey, they made for the MacPhedran Institute of Celtic Studies where Ruairidh showed them round the somewhat run-down Victorian building from which the institute operated. He introduced them to Jean, his secretary cum receptionist, who had on a number of occasions answered Richard's phone calls when seeking contact with the professor.

"I'm pleased to meet you at last and put a face to the voice. Ruairidh tells me that the place would fall apart without you."

She smiled, "Oh, I'm not so sure about that, but I do my best to keep the show going in this ramshackle old building. It's always in such a boorach. And this is Frances. I'm pleased to meet you and I hear that you have a job on your hands to keep these two adventurers from getting into trouble."

Frances admitted that this was so, but on this occasion, they were on holiday and were not planning any adventures.

Ruairidh agreed that adventures were not on the agenda and added:

"Jean is quite right about the building. This old place has served us well over the years, but it's past its best now. We have plans to move to the new university campus on the edge of town in the next couple of years. That should improve everyone's working conditions."

On departure from Ruairidh's office, Richard and Frances strolled round the pleasant Highland Capital's Old Town area and the Victorian Market with its quirky shops, after which they set off up the right bank of the crystal clear River Ness, crossed the river by a series of little white pedestrian suspension bridges linking the wooded Ness Islands. They returned to the city centre *via* the left bank and the famous multi-venue Eden Court Theatre. This they entered to explore and have a bite of lunch.

In the foyer, Frances lifted a leaflet from a rack.

"Look Richard: a programme for the Dualchas Festival that Ruairidh was talking about. And here's a picture of that Councillor MacLeod inside the front cover."

She read through the councillor's welcome and scanned the leaflet.

"Some good acts, and in places all over the Highlands too. And look: that Dale Campbell seems to be pretty prominent as fear an taighe[5] for some of the big events. He's on in Ullapool tonight and here in Eden Court tomorrow."

---

[5] Gaelic meaning master of ceremonies, literally man of the house, pronounced Fer an Te-ye.

Richard looked at the programme and then at Frances.

"We'll be away by the time he's in Inverness and in any case we couldn't possibly go while we are staying with Ruairidh. That would be a real a kick in the teeth for him, but . . . maybe when we're in Skye . . . Anyway, let's eat and after that we can see a bit more of Inverness and then head back to Ruairidh's place."

After lunch, the couple continued their exploration of the Highland capital, They were about to make for the shops to get some supplies for the forthcoming evening meal, which Frances had offered to prepare, when her iPhone rang. She looked at the display.

"It's Ruairidh."

"Hello Ruairidh . . . Yes . . . Oh that'll be fine . . . Yes, It'll be interesting to meet him . . . I think that should be all right, but I'll check with Richard."

"What was that about?"

"Well apparently a Norwegian Professor has called at his office and Ruairidh has asked him to stay the night. Do you remember Professor Einar Lund, from Oslo? He came to our spring conference at Dalmannoch and talked about Viking Paganism.

"Ah yes, I do remember – a rather solemn man, but quite a scholar."

"Yes. Well he's going to Skye tomorrow and Ruairidh wondered if we would give him a lift."

"Well I suppose that would be all right so long as you don't mind."

Frances had no objection and so the matter was agreed. Frances phoned Ruairidh to confirm the arrangement. Food was purchased and the Renault made its way back to Ruairidh's house with its spectacular loch-side view.

* * *

Roast leg of lamb followed by fruit salad had become something of a tradition with Frances when entertaining and the meal that evening was a success. After a few glasses of claret, the outwardly po-faced Professor Einar Lund opened up to contribute to a convivial evening.

It transpired that, having spent the previous few days at the university's Centre for Nordic Studies in Orkney, Professor Lund was now, like Richard and Frances, planning to visit Sabhal Mòr Ostaig[6], Scotland's unique Gaelic college located in the Isle of Skye. As Richard, Frances and Einar discussed the following day's journey to Skye, Ruairidh expressed regret.

"I wish I could go with you. The Sabhal Mòr is such an inspiring place. But the next couple of days are particularly busy for me. Then the girls will be here over the weekend. It's my best chance to spend quality time with them."

Frances sympathized.

"It would have been lovely if you could have joined us in Skye, but the girls come first. I'm only sorry we weren't able to meet them on this occasion."

---

[6] Pronounced Sawl <u>more</u> <u>Os</u>taig

RAVENBLACK

IT was Thursday morning. Everyone left Ruairidh's house simultaneously at half past eight. Ruairidh for the institute in Inverness; Frances, Richard and Professor Lund in the Megane westwards in the direction of the Isle of Skye.

Within an hour or so the yellow car had passed Cluaine Inn, crossed the great watershed of Druim Albann to proceed downhill through Glen Shiel, another of Scotland's spectacular mountain passes where towering crags seemed to envelop the travellers. As the road wound, twisted and descended, the River Shiel swelled and foamed as it was fed from white streaming cascades on either side of the glen. It had clearly been raining hard on this side of the country and a fine drizzle persisted as wisps of mountain mist draped the middle heights.

Frances was awe-struck.

"This is even more dramatic than Glen Coe."

"It's Homeric", agreed Richard.

Professor Lund also absorbed the prospect and likened it, rather matter-of-factly, to parts of his native Norway.

When the road eventually reached the west coast at Shiel Bridge, the travellers were further entranced by the splendour of the fjord-like Loch Duich along whose northern shore they proceeded until they came to that most romantic of Scottish icons – the sea-girt Eilean Donan Castle.

"Och look," exclaimed Frances, "Let's stop. It's just what a Scottish Castle *should* look like."

And so the little group parked the car at the visitor centre, which had just opened for the morning. They paid

£6.50 each and made their way across the causeway and stone bridge to the little island upon which the castle has stood since the 13th Century.

As they reached the studded door of the castle, a plaque read: *Fhad 'sa bhitheas MacRath a stigh, na bhitheadh Frisealach a muigh.* Frances translated this for the benefit of Einar: "So long as there is a MacRae within, let not a Fraser be outside".

As they puzzled the meaning of this, a young kilted guide approached them.

"The castle was founded to protect the area from Viking raids and was for centuries a stronghold of the Mackenzie's and their allies the MacRaes. The MacRaes came originally from the Fraser territory of Lovat, in the eastern part of the Highlands; hence the bond of kinship between the two clans."

He went on to explain that the castle was blown up in 1719 by Government forces after which it had been a ruin until reconstructed in the early twentieth century by Lieutenant-Colonel John Macrae-Gilstrap. The guide then ushered them into the banqueting hall – not huge or refined, but the grandest room in the castle and the epitome of a rough-hewn baronial hall – bare stone walls, arches, heraldry and ancestral portraits.

Frances was enthralled.

"Sure this is what I call interior decoration. Some ideas here for Dalmannoch?"

Richard was less captivated by baronial display.

"I think Frances, you are getting a mite carried away. First it was Inveraray Castle and now this Brigadoon. It is pretty impressive though, I must admit."

Einar kept his thoughts to himself.

Ascending to the battlements, notwithstanding the light drizzle, the trio took in the spectacular panorama of mountain and loch. The castle is in fact close to the confluence of three sea lochs – Loch Duich, Loch Long and Loch Alsh. Beyond lay the Isle of Skye. From this vantage point, Richard's eye was drawn to a small rigid inflatable boat lying at a jetty on the Ardelve shore opposite. A middle-aged man in a dark business suit was boarding the craft, aided by two yellow jacketed crewmen. A fourth man in a light grey business suit remained ashore and waited until the RIB backed away from the jetty and sped off seaward into Loch Alsh.

"Mm. I wonder what that was all about," muttered the ex-monk to no one in particular.

A voice behind him said:

"That RIB comes in here from time to time. They say it belongs to an outfit that's planning to install a tidal stream energy generating plant in or around the Sound of Sleat."

Richard turned round and the voice was that of their kilted guide.

"Sound of Sleat? Where's that?"

"Oh," responded the guide, "it's the stretch of water between Skye and the mainland. A fearful current runs through there at mid-water, which is, I suppose, what these guys are trying to tap. They're a pretty secretive bunch by all accounts."

"Interesting. I'd read something about tidal stream energy", acknowledged Richard, "but didn't realize people were actually developing it here in the West Highlands."

The guide nodded.

"Well, from what I hear, it's early days and there are major issues with grid connections and such like, but these people, whoever they are, seem to be up to something along these lines. I'm Iain Macrae by the way. I'm a history student and I suppose this tidal stream energy thing is history in the making."

With that, Frances thanked their young and informative guide, suggesting that it was time to head for Skye, and so the three of them made their way back to the car.

The drive from Eilean Donan Castle visitor centre to Kyle of Lochalsh, with its views over Loch Alsh and Skye, took just a quarter of an hour. By mutual consent a stop was made for toilets and coffee. Frances was mildly apologetic.

"We should have gone while we were at the Castle Visitor Centre. My fault for chivvying you."

The Norwegian professor came to her defence.

"No, this is fine. I'd quite like to have a look around here if that's all right now that the rain has more or less stopped."

Richard concurred, especially, as an ex-sailor, on seeing that there was evidence of maritime activity.

"Fine by me too Einar. Let's take a stroll."

Frances headed for the toilets and indicated that she wanted to explore the visitor centre and shops. The two men made for the Railway Pier, the terminus of the famed Kyle Railway with berthing alongside for fairly substantial vessels.

Of the two vessels berthed that day, one was a somewhat battered and rusty French trawler. In contrast, the other, taking on fuel, was a large, very smart, sleek and obviously very expensive motor yacht. She had a black hull with the upper-works in white and yellow detailing. The yacht flew a Norwegian ensign over her stern and a large house pennant from her mast. The pennant was yellow with, at the fly, a stylized black bird. The transom stern bore the legend:

        RAVNSVART
BERGEN

The name was flanked by symbols composed of what looked like interleaved triangles. Richard, although normally a devotee of more traditional craft, was captivated by the beauty and sheer panache of this elegant creation.

It was Professor Lund who spoke first.

"I know of this ship. It is owned by a very wealthy Norwegian businessman called Ragnar Torkelsen. He's a – how do you say – an enigma. He controls several companies mainly connected with the oil industry, but I read that he has recently moved into renewable energy."

As the two men walked further along the quay, an elaborate decoration came into view on the yacht's starboard shoulder. It was in the form of what to Richard looked like a grotesque parrot.

"That," explained the professor, "is a symbolic raven. The raven, you see, is closely associated with the Old Norse God Odin. And did you notice the triangle design on the stern. This is known as the Valknot, which means knot of the slain. This symbol is also associated with Odin and his power to bind or loosen the minds and souls of man, subtly affecting the knotted web of fate. And the ship's name – *Ravnsvart* – that means raven-black.

You see Ragnar Torkelsen is well known in Norway as a follower to the Old Norse Pagan religion. He's an Odinist."

As the two men pondered the provenance of this elegant vessel, a big and burly sailor appeared on deck to check progress with the intake of fuel. He wore black trousers and a black knitted gansey and baseball cap bearing the same raven design as featured on the house pennant.

Einar attempted conversation in Norwegian:

"*Morgen. Hvordan står det til?*"

The other looked round at the professor and replied with a matter of fact: "*Bare bra takk,*" and then continued with his surveillance.

The professor persevered by introducing himself and asking if Herr Torkelsen was aboard. To be answered with a blunt:

"*Nei*".

Further questioning as to the Norwegian magnate's movements were met by non-committal shrugs. Clearly the sailor had no wish to communicate any useful information. He soon excused himself politely and disappeared within.

Richard exchanged glances with Professor Lund.

"Not very forthcoming, eh?"

The professor nodded.

"No – I think he has been told not to speak to strangers. You know Ragnar Torkelsen has a reputation in Norway as – how do you say," the professor searched for the English word, "an – an – a recluse. He is very rich and successful, but most peoples thinks he has strange ideas – a little bit scary."

MISTY ISLE

THE two men walked back up the pier towards the village centre, each with his own thoughts about this mysterious but absent Norwegian and his fancy black motor yacht. They found Frances coming out of the tourist information office.

"Well boys, did you enjoy your little jaunt?" She didn't wait for an answer. "I've picked up some leaflets. We must go to Dunvegan Castle while we're in Skye – and Elgol, where there's a magnificent view of the Cullins, and Portree – and the Clan Donald Centre – that's almost next door to the Sabhal Mòr – and then . . ."

Richard held up his hand. "Okay, Okay, you win, but first we have to get to the Sabhal Mòr and check in ourselves. Then we can work out a schedule."

With that the trio returned to the car. Before setting off, sandwiches of cold lamb left over from the previous evening's meal were consumed. Thereafter, with Richard at the wheel, they headed for the Skye Bridge – a long slender concrete arch that soared across the narrow sound of Kyle Akin to land the travellers painlessly on the Isle of Skye. The Renault sped westwards in the direction of Broadford and then after a few miles, turned left and southwards towards Armadale and into the peninsula of Sleat – the Garden of Skye.

Richard noticed that he was doing eighty-five miles an hour and still accelerating. He eased his right foot's pressure off the accelerator.

"These roads are amazingly good. I somehow thought they would be narrow and twisty. This is more like a motorway, but with almost no traffic."

As if to demonstrate that theirs was not quite the only car on the road, a fast moving pick-up truck passed them in the opposite direction.

Frances looked around her at a scene of empty undulating moorland and, a little further to the right, noted the outline of high mountains wreathed in an ever changing pattern of mist. "I can see why they call this the Misty Isle. I hope the weather picks up though. The Rev says the scenery is breath-taking when the weather's fine."

Soon the scene changed to more pastoral, wooded and inhabited in character with, on the left, intermittent coastal views of the Sound of Sleat and the faint shape of the mountains of mainland Knoydart beyond. Onwards they drove through a series of crofting townships until, at length, they turned left down a short drive to behold a remarkable sight.

Ahead and to left and right, against a wild backdrop of sea, mountains and dark grey threatening sky, lay an array of futuristic white buildings quite unlike anything any of the trio had previously seen. This was the main campus of the famous and unique Gaelic college – Sabhal Mòr Ostaig.

A parking place was found and the little group made its way on foot the short distance to a little piazza where a welcome sign in Gaelic indicated that ahead, within the main building, was located the reception and also an eatery. The buildings to left and right were clearly living accommodation, as indicated by bed symbols, while the building further to the right was apparently something to do with creative and cultural businesses.

They entered the main building through a glass door to find themselves at a reception desk, beyond which was an atrium.

A young woman looked up and smiled from behind the desk and greeted them with a: "*Feasgar math.*[7]"

As the main language used within the college is Gaelic, the ensuing conversations were conducted in that language. They are translated as follows:

"Good afternoon." It was Frances who acted as spokesperson. She introduced Richard and Professor Lund and explained that they had been booked for the weekend Gaelic culture and history course.

"Ah yes surely, surely. We have been expecting you. Professor Ruairidh Macdonald has asked us to take good care of you. Pity about the weather, but they say we'll have a more settled day tomorrow. The course doesn't start until tomorrow evening, so you will have time to see something of our beautiful island. Just a minute and I'll get Eilidh to show you round."

She keyed a pad, spoke into her mike and after a few minutes a dark haired woman of perhaps thirty five appeared.

"Hello. I'm Eilidh Drummond. I'm lecturer in Celtic Studies. I'll be leading your course, but for now, I'll give you a brief tour of the college and then take you to your rooms."

And with that Eilidh took the group forward and down a stairway to a lower level and the servery and dining area. This formed the base of the atrium, the whole

---

[7] Gaelic pronounced <u>Fes</u> gar <u>mah</u>, meaning good afternoon

east wall of which was glass. It framed the same dramatic sea view that had been observed on arrival, except that the rocky foreshore was now visible close below.

The new arrivals were impressed. It was Frances who first gave voice.

"What a setting for a place of learning. It's inspirational."

Eilidh agreed and offered coffee or tea and biscuits which were gladly accepted. She then sat the little group down at a table near the great glass wall and summarized the origins and current functions of what was much more than just a college.

"It all started in the early nineteen seventies, when Iain Noble, an Edinburgh merchant banker, purchased substantial land holdings here in Skye. Among these scattered parcels of land was a dilapidated farm steading — Sabhal Mòr Ostaig, or the big barn of Ostaig. What was unusual about this new laird was that he had learnt to speak Gaelic fluently and he had a vision that the old steading should become a centre for the regeneration of the Gaelic language and culture — a college in other words providing vocational further education through Gaelic, together with a library and research facilities. In those early days, most people thought he was quite mad.

Anyway, in spite of the doubters, the old barn was made habitable and short courses commenced. Within a decade, accreditation to run full-time courses was achieved in what was the first college to run certified business, technology and other courses through the medium of the Scottish Gaelic language. From that small beginning the old steading was extended, and then it became clear that the site was too small to cope with ambitions for growth. A more substantial campus was required. Well the upshot was the brand new collection of buildings on this site. This new campus is now part of the University of the Highlands and Islands offering a full range of study, research and social activities from short weekend courses, such as the one you will attend, to full-time undergraduate and postgraduate degrees, and from musical and cultural events to research into Gaelic and Highland issues. So you see the vision of Sir Iain, as he became, was not so far-fetched after all."

Such was her enthusiasm that it was obvious Eilidh was very proud of the Sabhal Mòr, with its highly motivated personnel. By this point in her description, the little group had finished coffee.

A tour of the wondrous campus commenced. Eilidh explained that in earlier times, the fate of the local population was not such a happy one.

"Ever since the Union of the Scottish and English Crowns, many of the Highland chiefs, like others of the Scottish aristocracy and gentry, sought favour in the royal court in London. They needed money to finance their lavish lifestyles and, as a consequence, they sought to squeeze the last penny out of their Highland estates. One infamous act in 1739 by the First Baron Macdonald of Sleat, and his co-conspirator MacLeod of Dunvegan, was the kidnapping of men and women from their lands with the aim of selling them into slavery in North America. As it happened, the ship on which they were forced to sail was driven ashore by a storm in Donegal. Before the vessel could be made ready for sea again with its human cargo, local people heard the Gaelic voices of those within and the Highlanders were rescued. Many Donegal people today are descended from these refugees."

Frances was incensed.

"How awful for these people. I didn't realize Highland chiefs could be so cruel. And as a Donegal woman myself, now that I think about it, I know many a Macdonald among my friends, relations and neighbours. Maybe I'm even related to one of those unfortunates."

Eilidh continued:

"Could well be Frances, and in some ways these individuals were lucky. Who knows how many others were transported and worked to death as bond slaves on the other side of the Atlantic. By the early decades of the nineteenth century, later Macdonald chiefs sought to 'improve' their estates by adopting more profitable forms of land use such as rearing sheep. That is when this steading was built. There was no place for the tenants in this new order. They were simply evicted from their ancestral lands and their homes burnt down to prevent them returning. Some ended up in Canada, some in Glasgow or other cities and some simply died of starvation. So when these poor souls were herded to the coast they would have passed this new building under construction."

As Frances, Richard and Einar absorbed this gloomy account, Eilidh paused, gathered her thoughts and then explained:

"You see in those days virtually the whole population of the Highlands was Gaelic speaking — a carrying stream of millennia of rich Celtic culture. Then these widespread evictions, or clearances as we call them, followed by the Education Acts, which sought to extirpate Gaelic by punishing and humiliating children who spoke it, the disproportionate loss of young Highland men in two world wars and more recently the power of modern media, led to a steady decline in the numbers of Gaelic

49

speakers, to the point that extinction was thought to be inevitable.

It seems to me a delicious irony that this building, with its past role in destroying a community and a culture, has been a key tool in reversing the centuries old downward trend. Now with the development of Gaelic medium education, Gaelic television and a renaissance in Gaelic music and arts, the decline has been pretty well halted, as the growth of a new generation of confident young bi-lingual Gaelic speakers is now overtaking the deaths of the older generation. So, what the powers-that-be sought to destroy, we are now rebuilding."

Richard, Frances and even Einar were humbled by Eilidh's juxtaposition of cruel suppression of the native Gaelic culture of the Highlands and the efforts by which this wrong was gradually being righted through by who knows how many hundreds of committed individuals.

Eilidh took charge again.

"Well time is getting on. I'd better show you to your quarters. I hope you like them."

They retraced their steps, picked up their luggage from the car and made their way to the round tower at the northern edge of the campus.

"This is where you will stay for the next few days."

Eilidh ushered the group into the building and a lift where she pressed the button. To their surprise, the voice in the lift addressed them in Gaelic. On reaching the top floor Eilidh explained:

"Professor Macdonald asked us to put you into our two penthouse suites." Eilidh rummaged in her bag. "Professor Lund, here is the key for your accommodation and Brother Richard and Sister Frances, here is yours. I think you'll be happy here. I'll leave you for now, but if you need anything, just contact me at reception. Dinner will be served in about an hour's time."

And so Einar, Richard and Frances took occupation of their respective apartments, each of which had a balcony with magnificent views in all directions.

Standing on the balcony, Frances gave Richard a big hug.

"Oh Richard this is lovely, isn't it? Look, the mist's clearing. You can see for miles down the coast and across the water."

Hugging Frances, Richard agreed. They kissed, lingered for a couple of minutes and gazed once more to seaward.

Richard's nautical eye was attracted by a vessel making its way southwards at speed quite close to the shore.

"Look Francie. That's the same Norwegian yacht Einar and I saw at Kyle."

Richard reached for his binoculars and focused them on the sleek vessel. On the yacht's flying bridge was a dark clad bearded figure wearing a pilot jacket and skipper's peaked cap. He too had binoculars to his eyes and seemed to be scanning the college intently. Then Richard sensed that he had been spotted. The mysterious mariner's binoculars fixed on the accommodation tower's penthouse balcony for half a minute, after which they were lowered and, with a final glance, he turned his attention to his vessel's direction of travel.

"Mm. I suppose that must have been Ragnar Torkelsen. I wonder why he was so interested in the Sabhal Mòr.

DALMANNOCH AFFAIRS

WHILE Brother Richard, Frances and the Norwegian professor made their way to the Gaelic college, two individuals in the south west of Scotland were shaken by a strange turn of events.

Holly Garden had shared the night in the bed of John Walker — Donnelly Dolan's roadie whom everyone knew as Whisky. As the morning light stirred her from her dreams, she marvelled at how cosy the mobile home's double bed was. She leant on one arm to study Whisky's good humoured and lived-in face. He was breathing the steady breath of a man still in contented slumber. She kissed his brow.

He stirred, half opened his eyes, smiled at this older woman who had bewitched him. Witchcraft or not, he was happier and more relaxed than he had been for many a day. He closed his eyes again and slid back into a pleasant dose.

Holly rose, put on a kettle and five minutes later brought back two mugs of tea — Earl Grey — that was what Whisky liked to waken with first thing. He stirred again, propped himself up against the headboard to embrace the welcome cup.

Holly slid back between the covers beside him. There, propped up side by side, they supped, naked, touching and content in each other's silence.

Holly, in reverie, looked back on her life. As a girl she had been fey, but at the age of twenty one, convention called, or so she thought. She had married Clive Garden, a supermarket under manager. Things seemed all right at first although the physical side of the marriage had been less exciting than she had been led to expect. Then after three years Clive announced that he was gay and was moving out. He and his friend George moved to Manchester to set up a gay bar and that was the last she saw of her husband.

This had been a blow to Holly's self-esteem. In the aftermath she had let herself go, but in time she discovered that she had special gifts that others valued — gifts of healing and wisdom, but also the, at times disconcerting, gift of seeing. Then some seven years back, she had met former marine, Thomas Nutter who, himself had come through bad times and who introduced her to the Wicca movement. This led to the founding of the Wigtown Wicca Coven, of which she became priestess and found herself valued for herself. The relationship with Thomas was close in its way, but not romantic. So all the while the pleasure of sex had passed her by, until Whisky arrived on the scene.

Whisky was so different. Holly learnt that in his young life, he had done the sex, drugs, rock and roll scene and come through it to become a steadying influence on the talented, but wayward Donnelly Dolan. Whisky had turned his back on drugs, drank little if any alcohol, pursued a moderate and mainly vegetarian diet and exercised regularly. Sex was another matter. He had had a number of steady girlfriends and countless one-night-stands. The pressures and temptations of the road had not been conducive to long term relationships. While on tour it seems, girls threw themselves at him and he and they took their mutual enjoyment of the moment.

On the first night of the Dalmannoch Music Festival, Whisky had ended up in bed with Sadie Sim, but, thereafter, Sadie had latched on to one of the Bluegrass Boys, so that by the second evening of the festival, a stroll with Holly in the Dalmannoch wood had led to a kiss, a cuddle, a more passionate kiss, a mutual fondling, exploration and the best sex Holly had ever experienced.

Such was the boost to her morale that by the end of the festival, with Whisky's encouragement, Holly had gone for a complete makeover of hair, clothes and make-up.

Whisky's uninhibited promiscuity fascinated Holly. It was by no means at odds with her belief in the Wiccan read: "If it harm none — do as ye will". In fact it unleashed a hitherto dormant passion and she was glad to be included in Whisky's pantheon of lovers. She had taken a fancy to him at first sight. It was partly his well-toned body and easy manner, but also something deeper and more spiritual. She was frankly astonished that he had picked up on her feelings and, despite her being so much older, and a bit on the plump side, he had responded, firstly in exploring an interest in, and curiosity about, her spiritual path.

Both were Pagans, but of different kinds. Holly's Wiccan rite was characterized mainly by gentleness and empathy with nature, especially human nature. Whisky, on the other hand, had been accepted into something altogether more elemental and hard-edged — the belief system of the Vikings. These Norsemen of old were ruthless, cunning and, yes, bloodthirsty, but in their own way they respected valour, justice and Fate.

As Whisky set out the Odinist creed, based on the nine noble virtues of courage, truth, honour, fidelity, discipline, hospitality, self-reliance, industriousness and perseverance, Holly was at once fearful and entranced. Whisky and his spiritual path had opened her eyes to a whole new level of Pagan experience. Of course, Whisky explained, that unlike the free ranging Vikings of old, modern Odinists keep a low profile and live within the law.

* * *

In bed that morning, a few weeks after their first meeting, Whisky turned to Holly, and with a gentle kiss, whispered;

"Good morning lover girl."

For all she knew, Whisky said that to all the girls he bedded, but no matter, she liked being called a girl. It made her feel young.

"Good morning my big hairy Viking."

Kisses, cuddles and sex, and then they were set for the day.

After showers and breakfast, Whisky switched on his iPad to check messages. As he scrolled through message by message separating the dross from the relevant, Holly watched, enjoying the quiet, efficient manner in which her lover dealt with the day to day business of a roadie cum manager handling queries, noting future gig opportunities, reassuring contacts. It all seemed so effortless, although Holly knew it was not.

And then a frown.

Whisky seemed to read and re-read one particular message.

"I don't like the look of this."

"What is it my love."

Whisky looked at Holly with what almost looked like fear in his eyes.

Holly, concerned, asked again. "What's wrong?"

Whisky was silent for a couple of minutes. Then he felt the need to share his concern with this woman he loved and trusted.

"Can you promise not to say anything about this to anyone?"

"I promise John. What is it?"

"Well," Whisky paused to gather his thoughts. "It's from my Norwegian pal, Anders Anderssen. He's a member of the Brigen Odinist Hearth in Bergen. He's sent me a message about the most powerful of all Norway's Odinists — a very rich and secretive tycoon called Ragnar Torkelsen. I met him once. He's kind of quiet, but messianic. Well, Anders says, he's cruising round the Scottish islands in his yacht."

Whisky paused again.

Holly looked at him, puzzled.

"Why the secret? Surely that's innocent enough. Lots of well-off people cruise round the Scottish islands."

Whisky returned Holly's look.

"Yes, normally — normally — yes but, according to Anders, Ragnar Torkelsen is on a death moot."

"What does that mean?"

"It means that he has gone off to fight some great evil that will end with either his own death or the death of his enemy. Anders wants me to keep an eye on him. Meantime I have to await further instructions."

"Well," said Holly defiantly, "if you're gallivanting after bezerker Vikings, so am I."

O N the morning after their arrival in Skye, the weather cleared. Einar had arranged to meet up with a fellow academic to discuss some esoteric aspect of Norse place names in the Western Highlands and Islands. Brother Richard and Frances, however, had time on their hands and did what a million first time visitors to Skye have done before them. They explored the sights — picturesque Portree, the island capital, Dunvegan Castle, home of the clan chief MacLeod of MacLeod, Elgol with its view of the rugged Cullins and the Clan Donald Centre.

The last named place was of special interest. There they learned about the mightiest of all the clans, Clan Donald which had ruled a vast Gaelic maritime kingdom — the Kingdom and later the Lordship of the Isles. This realm had its origins in the time when the Vikings ruled almost all of the islands stretching from Shetland and Orkney in the north to the Hebrides in the west and the Isle of Man in the south. Then with the defeat of the Norwegian King Haakon at the battle of Largs in 1263, Mann and the Hebrides were ceded to Scottish control, a control that was so tenuous, however, that the Macdonald Lords of the Isles were effectively independent princes in their own right.

Back at the college for the evening meal, three other course arrivals were at the dinner table. Each in their own way attracted the attention of one or other of Richard, Frances and Einar.

Mark Curno was from Cornwall, a speaker of the Cornish language and a bard of the Cornish Gorsedh. He was keen to learn about how Scottish Gaelic fared, as compared with his own Celtic language.

Richard was intrigued. "My mother was Cornish. She hailed from Newlyn. I have very fond memories of summer holidays there with my relations when I was a boy."

And with that an animated discussion commenced between Mark and Richard.

As this was in progress, Frances introduced herself to a middle-aged woman sitting opposite. She was Sinead Ni Branáin from Dingle in the south west of Ireland. This time their mutual Irish origins sparked off an exploration of each other's background and interests.

The third new arrival was Chuck McColl, from North Carolina, whose distant Highland ancestors had fetched up there in the eighteenth century. For a time, he and Einar simply listened to the flow of conversation among the others, until they too found a mutual interest in Native American shamanism. The separate conversations soon morphed into a wide-ranging multi-faceted communal debate.

Just as they were finishing their main course, Eilidh appeared and came up to the table. She seemed preoccupied, but attempted a smile.

"You know the course starts at seven thirty in the small lecture room. You've got quarter of an hour. There'll be coffee and biscuits in the room. Quite a few other participants have already arrived."

She paused, as if gathering her thoughts, and then revealed her concern.

"I'm afraid we have all had a bit of a shock. Yesterday, two of our students found a body on the shoreline up the coast from here. We've just heard that

the deceased was one of our local politicians —
Councillor Ewan Allan MacLeod. We are all very
distressed. You see, he was particularly supportive of the
college."

It was Frances who asked how Councillor
MacLeod had died, to which Eilidh replied.

"Nobody seems to know the circumstances as yet.
It looks as though he drowned. His wife had to go to
Inverness today to identify the body."

The group sympathized with her concern about
this unfortunate event, but Eilidh changed the subject and
urged them to make their way to the small lecture room.

There were another dozen or so folk assembled
there hovering over the coffee and tea, munching biscuits
and making mutual introductions. Some were staying in
local hotels or guest houses, the rest were local residents
who were clearly regulars at the Sabhal Mòr's weekend
courses.

At seven thirty, Eilidh called the group to order
and introduced Doctor Kenneth MacFarlane as their
lecturer. Eilidh departed and the evening's proceedings
commenced with an overview of early European Celtic
civilizations. He was engaging, well informed and, by the
end of this first session at nine o'clock, all agreed that the
week-end course promised to be worthwhile.

* * *

The following morning, Saturday, at breakfast
Eilidh appeared again with more news about the body
which had been found two days before. She conveyed the
fresh intelligence that the police were treating Councillor
MacLeod's death as murder.

Normally, this news would have been regarded by the study participants as no more than sensational local gossip that had little bearing on their own lives. As far as Richard and Frances were concerned, however, the matter was to become more personal, for, after the morning class, just as lunch was about to be served, the Reverend Donald Angus MacLeod appeared.

The Rev, as most at Dalmannoch called him, was highly regarded by Richard and Frances. When they had last seen him a week before at the trustees' meeting, he had been in high spirits, still buoyed up by the success of the music festival, but also delighted that Richard and Frances had planned to visit the Highlands and Islands and especially his native Isle of Skye.

Now his mood was sombre.

Richard grasped the Rev's hand in both of his. "Donald, what a surprise, and good to see you?"

"Lovely to see you both too. I'm afraid I have had some bad news. My brother Ewan Allan has died. It seems he was murdered – an awful business. My sister-in-law Shona phoned me yesterday from Inverness, after the *post mortem*, to let me know. I dropped everything and drove up last night. I'll be staying with Shona in Broadford until after the funeral."

Frances hugged Donald. "I'm so sorry Donald. We heard about the – er – Councillor MacLeod's death yesterday and then Eilidh told us this morning that murder was suspected. How awful for you. We were just saying that you told us a while back that you had a brother in Skye who was a councillor. We wondered if Councillor MacLeod was – well, you know – the same man. Oh dear. How sad."

Donald nodded and muttered thanks for their kind thoughts, whereupon Richard ushered the three of them to a small table separate from the main group and suggested lunch. Donald was well known at the college, having in the past taught both Gaelic and piping at summer courses and for him lunch was on the house.

Over the meal Donald described his relationship with his brother and how their lives had taken different paths, although both had ended up in their separate ways as public figures.

"You see, Ewan, as the elder son, was the favoured one. He stood to inherit the family croft and always had an easy ride. I can't say he kept to the straight and narrow path of righteousness, but then none of us are saints. I needn't go into his failings, but what I do know and respect is that he was fundamentally a man of honour. I know that as a councillor he fought hard to ease the plight of many a poor soul who was being unfairly treated.

He's – sorry – he *was* something of a visionary too. He was a staunch supporter of this college and of the Gaelic language and was well regarded here. He also had been very keen for some time to see the strong tidal flows between Skye and the Mainland exploited for generating "green" electricity. In fact he chaired a council sub-committee that has been working on the idea with the Scottish Government and the Crown Estates who control the sea bed. Apparently there is huge potential for tapping tidal stream energy round the Scottish coasts, if the technology can be perfected and the economics made to stack up. Apparently the prize is enormous and those who crack the know-how and get in early are likely to make a lot of money.

"Bearing in mind our rather separate lives, Ewan and I didn't communicate much, but the strange thing is that he phoned me this Monday evening to say that he was worried.

"He had been approached by two different companies about a particular development of tidal stream energy here in Skye and was being pressurized to favour one of them against the other. As a councillor, he is of course duty bound to remain neutral regarding any commercial dealings and I know Ewan would abhor accepting financial inducements to influence his judgment. He didn't go into detail, but said he had agreed to a meeting the following morning to try to confront one or other of them. I don't know who these outfits are, but I could tell Ewan was scared."

Richard and Frances listened to Donald's revelations and then Richard spoke.

"You must be feeling awful about this, Donald. I'm really sorry about your troubles."

Frances added: "And Shona, your sister-in-law – Ewan's wife?" Donald nodded. "How is she coping? It must have hit her hard."

"Well yes. I think she hasn't quite taken it all in yet, but she seems to be bearing up in the circumstances."

There was a silence for a couple of minutes as each was lost in though. Then Richard mentioned the chance encounter a few days before on the ferry at which the Argyll Councilor Angus MacPhedran had told them about Councillor MacLeod's outburst at the government meeting in Edinburgh where renewable energy had been mentioned.

"How did MacPhedran describe it? – 'Yanks?! Muscling in where they're not wanted. And bloody

Vikings! We threw *them* out hundreds of years ago. They'll make a comeback over my dead body!' These may not be his exact words, but it was something like that."

There was another brief silence and then Donald gave voice.

"A strange coincidence that; your meeting this MacPhedran chap who was at the same meeting as Ewan; and him mentioning it to you. But then I suppose they were both councillors and news, or should I say gossip, travels fast in the Highlands. The thing that strikes me is, maybe your account bears out Ewan's phone call to me. I wonder if the Yanks and Vikings, as he described them, were his take on the factions that he had been dealing with. Seems likely, doesn't it?"

There was agreement that this did indeed seem likely.

Donald rose from the table.

"Well I'd better be going. There's quite a lot to attend to. The police are calling at Shona's this afternoon. I'll mention the matter that Councillor MacPhedran raised with you. It might be helpful to them. All that aside it was good to meet up with you both and I'm glad you made it to our beautiful island and to the Sabhal Mòr. It is rather special isn't it?"

As he made his departure, Donald announced. "There is a Gaelic service in Broadford tomorrow evening at 6 o'clock. You might like to come along. There will be a short tribute to Ewan."

And so Richard and Frances were left to rejoin the other course participants to learn about the effects and intrigues of the Jacobite risings and their tragic effect on the fate of the Gaelic speaking people.

As they went into the lecture room, Richard remarked: "You know Francie, after what we discussed with Donald, it feels a bit as though foul deeds in these parts are not wholly a thing of the past."

ON the west coast of Canada, Hector Woodrow Douglas had uncovered some disturbing information about who was behind the raid on his company's trading activities.

After Luigi Cassani had been escorted from the Vancouver head office of Woodrow Douglas Logistics, his room was locked, pending further investigations into his misdeeds. These misdeeds were reported immediately to the Vancouver Police Department, whose Financial Crime Unit took up the case. Officers of the unit inspected and took duplicate copies of Cassani's incriminating computer files and such few paper documents as seemed relevant. The key police contact was Sergeant Harry McColl, polite and sympathetic, but who explained to Hector, James and their legal adviser, Eustace Blake, that criminal fraud cases were often complex and that Woodrow Douglas Logistics may in the end be advised to seek redress in the civil courts as an alternative, or be referred to another agency depending on circumstances. The unit would, however, do its best to secure a positive outcome.

In the meantime Hector, his son James and other senior members of the firm, continued the process of explaining recent difficulties to clients and sought to placate those who had been misled or inconvenienced and to reestablish confidence. This took time and there was no doubt damage had been done to the company's reputation.

One particularly tricky negotiation was with Shaun Murphy, the boss of the Vancouver Chapter of the Longshore Workers' Union. Once the deliberate and damaging misrepresentation carried out by Cassani had been explained and demonstrated to be fabricated, however, even the hardline Murphy conceded that a line had been crossed and that it was certainly not in his members' interest for the firm to go out of business. Peace was restored and even a new mutual understanding and spirit of cooperation established.

Then when Luigi Cassani's body was taken from False Creek, the police were of the opinion that this had been a straightforward case of suicide. They saw no reason to suspect homicide and, after all, he was jobless and in all likelihood facing a goodly spell in prison.

Hector was not convinced about the matter of suicide. Luigi Cassani had clearly been working under instructions from someone else, someone unknown, someone presumably connected with the Whiteman organization. Was it possible that his 'suicide' had been set up, to prevent him talking? There was that sheet of paper, still in Hector's possession, with the 'ILLUMINATI' heading and words:

Succeed and you will be rewarded
You know the price of failure

Was death the price of failure? And what was this Illuminati thing about?

Hector shared his thoughts with his son.

"It may take long enough for the cops to come up with anything on who was behind Cassani now that he's dead. I think we should do a bit of digging ourselves. Let's start with his room."

And so that evening, after most of the workforce had left, Hector and James unlocked Cassani's room and a thorough search commenced. James checked the computer, but there was nothing unexpected, as his emails were now being automatically forwarded to the company's accounts department. Hector went through the desk drawers and the filing cabinet systematically. There didn't seem to be anything incriminating – papers and the usual office paraphernalia – pens, markers, calculator, stapler, paper clips, keys, business cards and such like. One of the business cards carried the name of an Eva Tillotson, Corporate Affairs Directorof Whitelite Power Inc., with an address in Wilmington, North Carolina. On the back were the words written in ball point, "keep up the good work Luigi".

"Look at this James, isn't Whitelite a subsidiary of Whiteman?"

Just as James was examining the card, the office door opened and the smiling young Filipino cleaner Adora Flores appeared, and made a slight bow.

"Sir, I saw that the light was on and wondered if I should clean Mr Cassani's room. I haven't been able to. It has been locked since he left."

Hector smiled back at this petite and helpful young woman:

"Ah thank you Adora. That won't be necessary for now. We'll let you know when it'll be free for cleaning, once we have found some important papers".

The cleaner bowed again and made her exit, and then returned a few seconds later looking slightly embarrassed:

"I – I'm sorry to interrupt you again Sir, but Mr Cassani often worked late, and a few weeks ago he asked me to keep a box in the cleaners' lock up. He said he didn't want it lying around in his office. Would you like me to get it?"

Hector and James looked at each other.

"Yess," they agreed in unison. Thank you."

They followed Adora to the cleaners' mess-room, wherein was located a built-in closet. A key was produced from a desk drawer and the closet door opened to reveal several shelves holding an assortment of items from step-ladders, bottles and tins of special and possibly toxic cleaning materials, to instruction manuals, protective clothing and on the top shelf a grey locked metal box. Adora reached up and lifted the box down and handed it to Hector.

"Thank you Adora, I think this may well be what we were looking for."

Adora smiled and gave another little bow:

"You are most welcome Sir, please let me know if I can be of further assistance."

Father and son returned with the box to Cassani's office and placed it on the desk.

"Now let's try some of these keys . . . No, not that one . . . Or these . . . Or that . . . Ah ha, this looks more like it. – Yesss – Bingo!"

And with a twist of the key the box was open.

"Now let's see what treasures are within."

Hector pulled out an assortment of papers.

"Now what have we here? – Mmm – letters – photographs – bank statements – mortgage schedule – bits and pieces . . ."

The pair examined the assemblage. Instinctively Hector focused on the financial statements.

"Look at this, James. It seems Cassani was up against it financially. The mortgage on his house was well over $3,000 a month and he was overdrawn."

Hector perused the documentation further.

"Mmm, this is interesting. Here's a sum of $20,000 credited to his account a month ago. That cleared the overdraft – very convenient. I wonder if we can find out where that came from."

Among the letters, some were old and written in Italian, dating back to the 1940s and 50s. Many of the snapshots seemed to be of that vintage too, or perhaps older, black and white, presumably of relatives – grandparents perhaps, uncles, aunts – who knows? There were a few more up-to-date colour photos – Cassani with a glamorous dark-haired bikini-clad female, another of him in the company of a man dressed in a business suit, apparently at some function or celebration. Among the other documentation were letters from the bank, divorce papers dating from the previous year from his (ex) wife Maria, utility bills and other routine correspondence, but, it seemed, nothing incriminating.

James summed up the situation.

"Well Dad, I'd guess his divorce was the origin of his financial problems. A payoff by whoever was trying to undermine our company must have seemed like an easy way out of the fix he was in. I suppose that's where the $20,000 came from, and presumably with more to follow when they had achieved their goal."

James's father nodded.

"Let's take this stuff home for safe keeping," and then he pondered, and smiled a slightly wicked smile. "You know what, ma boy. I think we should pay a visit to Cassani's house."

"What! break in?"

"No, breaking in will not be required." Hector held up a ring with two keys on it. "I'm pretty sure this is his house key." He then waved the instruction sheet for the house security alarm, on which the code was written in ink. "Let's go."

Cassani had lived in a row town-house in the up-market Mount Pleasant area of the city, on a side street a couple of blocks back from Broadway Avenue.

Within half an hour father and son, tried the key in the lock of Cassani's front door and they were in. With the aid of a flashlight they quickly found the alarm control box, keyed in the number and the system was disabled.

"Whew. Just as well Cassani hadn't changed the code. Now, let's draw the drapes and put the lights on."

With the lights on, the pair rummaged through drawers, firstly in the lounge-diner, and then in the bedrooms. At last, in a bedside cabinet James found a plain envelope. It contained a small sheet of paper and a DVD disc.

"Ah ha, look at this Dad."

The paper was headed with the same pyramid symbol underscored by the word 'ILLUMINATI', as on the scrap they had found in Cassani's work desk. It bore the further motto, *Ad majorem noster gloriam*. There was no address or contact information, just text.

The next steps in achieving our global purpose

Objective A: Suppress interest rates
Current action: Manipulate the Fed money supply

Objective B: Dominate China Pacific logistics
Current action: Capture Woodrow Douglas China traffic

Objective C: Control European tidal stream energy
Current action: Clinch Torkelsen Ravngen deal, Scotland.

"Well," exclaimed Hector, "at least this confirms that Cassani was acting under instructions to destroy us. But who the Hell are the Illuminati, Torkelsen and Ravngen?

ILLUMINATI

O N leaving the Sabhal Mòr, the Reverend Donald Angus MacLeod made his way to Shona MacLeod's guest house. Thus far, Shona was coping with the death of her husband by keeping busy attending to her duties as a guest house landlady. The Glasgow electricians were still present, but the German motor cyclists had left. Of course Donald was lodging with his sister-in-law.

Shona had always been fond of Donald – so different from her talented and, in many ways respected, but wayward and hard drinking husband.

Over a pot of tea, Donald did his best to comfort Shona, although he himself also felt the sudden and tragic loss of his brother just as much as Shona. The conversation naturally took place in Gaelic, which language was always more intimate and expressive of the familial bond. The strain lessened a little as the pair started to reminisce about "the old days" when life seemed lighter and more hopeful.

As they were thus engaged, the door-bell rang. On investigation, two policemen, Inspector MacGillivray and Sergeant Nicolson, stood there seeking entry. Shona showed them into the lounge and offered tea, which was accepted with thanks.

On returning carrying a tray laden with teapot, cups, milk, sugar and cakes, Shona introduced Donald.

"This is my husband's – er – my late husband's brother, the Reverend Donald Angus Macleod. I hope you don't mind him being present. He has been very supportive."

Inspector MacGillivray nodded and explained that they had been seeking to identify Councillor MacLeod's movements since he had last been seen by Shona, until the time of his death. They had issued a media appeal to the public to come forward with any information they may have regarding the councillors movements. They claimed to have made some progress, but wished to fill in gaps. Councillor MacLeod's wallet and diary had been retrieved from his suit, although his mobile phone was missing. The diary entries for the days in question had been cryptic. Although smudged by the effect of sea water, they gave some clue as to his intended movements."

Inspector MacGillivray showed Shona and Donald the relevant page.

Monday: 11:00 Islands wkg gp
Wednesday: 19:30 Fèis UL

"We met with the Council's Chief Executive. He confirmed that he had discussed with Councillor MacLeod the previous week the proposed licensing and planning consent for sea bed and adjacent land for the development of tidal power arrays in and around Loch Alsh and the Sound of Sleat. It seems that your husband was concerned about which potential operator might be in the frame. The two contenders are apparently a Norwegian company called, let me see, (the inspector consulted his notebook) ah yes, called Ravngen and an American developer called Whitelite Power. We are following up enquiries with these companies.

"The Council's Chief Executive confirmed that your husband was scheduled to attend an inter-authority meeting in Edinburgh on Monday and we subsequently checked that on the Wednesday evening he officiated at a musical event in Ullapool starring Dale Campbell. After that the trail goes cold. His car is still in Ullapool. How he fetched up in Camas Cross remains a mystery for the present. From his Visa card account, the Royal Caledonian Bank were able to confirm, after some persuasion, that he had paid for hotel accommodation in Aberdeen for Tuesday night and diesel fuel the following day. The hotel is in the Tullos area of the city, which is predominantly a large industrial and business estate devoted to the oil and gas industry and general services. We have circulated Councillor MacLeod's official council photograph and the Aberdeen police are checking with the hotel to see if anyone can remember him or any contacts he may have made. We have also asked the Kyle Harbour Master to check with local mariners and any other shipping movements around the time of your husband's death to see if anyone saw anything suspicious. We haven't come up with any positive leads as yet, but enquiries are still on-going.

"If either of you can help us to fill in some of the blanks, we would be most grateful."

Shona said that she would look through her husband's papers to see if she could find anything useful.

Donald butted in, mentioning Counellor MacLeod'outburst about "Yanks and bloody Vikings" at the Edinburgh meeting as reported by Councillor MacPhedran to Brother Richard. He then reiterated:

"Ewan phoned me on Monday evening to say that he was worried, as he had been approached by two different companies about tidal stream energy here in Skye and was being pressed to favour one of them against

74

the other. I know Ewan wouldn't accept a bribe and would resist being unduly influenced. In fact, knowing him, he would be inclined to stick his heels in out of bloody mindedness and defy such an approach. But he did say he had arranged a meeting to try to confront one or other of the interested parties. He didn't go into any more detail, but he sounded quite disturbed, threatened even. From what you have told us, Inspector, it would seem that the reason he was in Aberdeen was to have this confrontation."

Inspector MacGillivray listened with interest. "Mm – interesting. Thank you Reverend MacLeod, most helpful. That does rather confirm some connection between these tidal energy developments and your brother's death. I think we should have a word with Councillor MacPhedran and with this Brother Richard."

Donald Angus added helpfully. "No doubt you will find Councillor MacPhedran through Argyll and Bute Council, but Richard Wells and his good lady are here in Skye attending a course at the Sabhal Mòr. I believe they will be coming along to the Gaelic service in Broadford tomorrow evening and assembling here beforehand."

The inspector and sergeant thanked Shona and the Reverend for their help, asked them to contact the police if they uncovered any other information that might be helpful and left in the direction of the Kyle Harbour Master's office.

* * *

The harbour master had been diligent in identifying vessels and mariners who were around at, and before, the supposed time of Councillor MacLeod's death.

His verbal report to Inspector MacGillivray and Sergeant Nicolson was to the point.

"There were several vessels in the area on Thursday morning. Here at the Railway Pier, the trawler *Amitié* of Boulogne has been berthed for the last week. Her skipper, Captain Vincent Garnier, has gone to France to meet with the owners. Apparently there are some financial problems. I have spoken with the mate, a surly bugger called Georges Dupont, and he claims to have seen nothing untoward, nor, he says, did any others of the crew. From my schoolboy French I understand the ship's name means 'friendship', particularly ill-named if you ask me. You might be able to get more information than I could.

"Then there was a fancy Norwegian motor yacht. Now what was the name?" The harbour master consulted his log. "Ah yes *Ravnsvart* from Bergen. She came in from Ullapool that morning at 08:45 and took on bunkers. She left again heading south at 14:10. Where she is now I couldn't say, but if it's important we can find out from AIS."

The inspector interrupted. "AIS?"

"Ah yes," the harbour master explained, "automatic identification system – it's a satellite tracking system that shows the identification, position, course, and speed of any registered vessel anywhere in the world."

The inspector pondered: "It might be useful to know where that Norwegian yacht is now."

"Then there was the Naval service tender *Trusty*. She left the Kyle base at 08:05 northwards in the direction of Applecross on torpedo testing duties. She would have passed *Ravnsvart* on her southbound approach to Kyle. I haven't spoken with her commanding officer."

The harbour master then continued:

"There was another ship in the general vicinity – a survey and supply vessel *Whiteman Pioneer*. She's been around these parts before – something to do with tidal energy development for an American outfit called Whitelite Power. She was reported to be in Loch Alsh on Thursday morning and according to Lachie Mackinnon, a local fisherman, who was checking his lobster creels in that area, she was anchored for a time by the Glenelg shore. There was also a RIB dashing back and forth to various marker buoys and such like. Then about midday, according to Lachie, *Whiteman Pioneer* lifted her hook and set off southwards past Kylerhea and into the Sound of Sleat. We can find her current position too if needs be.

"That's about it. If I hear any more, I'll let you know."

Inspector MacGillivray expressed gratitude to the harbour master for the trouble he had taken in assembling this information and Sergeant Nicolson closed his notebook, having completed a summary of these maritime activities.

As the two officers walked back to the police car, the Sergeant spoke.

"Bit of a coincidence Sir, that Norwegian yacht coming from Ullapool to Kyle, when the last place we knew of Councillor MacLeod alive the night before was Ullapool."

The inspector pondered.

"You may be on to something there Stevie. We should definitely make contact with – what's the name of the boat?"

"*Ravnsvart*".

"Yes, that's the fellah. And we'd better check up on that *Whiteman* what's it too. It was in the vicinity and the crew may have seen something."

After the police had departed, the harbour master checked the positions of the two vessels in question on AIS. He ascertained that *Whiteman Pioneer* was at Mallaig and *Ravnsvart* was berthed at Leverburgh at the south end of Harris in the Outer Hebrides. This information was conveyed to Inspector MacGillivray.

THE SABBATH

THERE was a time, not so distant, in the Presbyterian Highlands and Islands, when nothing moved on a Sunday; nothing that is, aside from the solemn trudge of the faithful to and from church, a trudge all the more solemn if accompanied by wind and rain – a not infrequent occurrence. The Lord's Day was for the Lord and no one else. Public transport by land, sea or air did not function, children's swings were chained up and even the cockerels, it is said, were caged, in case the day of rest was violated by unseemly ardour. And any outward signs of pleasure or frivolity were considered unseemly. What went on behind closed doors and drawn curtains was perhaps another matter. The ultra-sanctimonious seemed at times to be blessed by numerous children.

Churches vied as to which was the holiest. In 1843, the Free Church had split from the Church of Scotland and the Free Church tended to take a stricter line on Sunday observance than the Old Kirk, which was itself then strict enough. In 1893, not to be outdone, the even stricter Free Presbyterians broke away from the Free Church. Few can now remember why, but whatever the reason, it must have been important at the time.

Such attitudes were, and to an extent remain, a phenomenon of Presbyterianism. Schisms and regroupings of this kind continue to this day. Traditionally Catholic communities, in places like Barra, South Uist and Moidart, took a more relaxed and pragmatic approach to Sundays. By the latter part of the twentieth century, however, despite the best efforts of ministers to resist change, change came. The advent of the washing machine and tumble drier, which could be utilized, unseen by outside eyes, on any day of the week, meant that the highly visible scandal of putting out washing on a Sunday could be averted. The appearance of Sunday observance could be maintained even although its practice may have been diluted by the whirring kitchen appliances and the flicker of the unholy television in the corner of the living room. Then even appearances went by the board, when, in 1965, notwithstanding the Reverend Angus Smith lying down on the slipway in front of the ferry's vehicle ramp, Skye was, for the first time, served by ferries on Sundays. By the dawn of the twenty-first century even Lewis and Harris, Scotland's last redoubt of Sabbatarianism, succumbed to Sunday ferries.

It was in the light of this history that Richard and Frances were curious to attend a Gaelic Church service, which they were informed retained many of the features of Presbyterian worship formerly prevalent, but now lost elsewhere. In time-honored fashion, that Sunday had been one of a light but persistent drizzle. Skye was once again living up to its by-name *Eilean a' Cheo* — the Isle of Mist.

Having spent the day on course work at the Sabhal Mòr, Richard and Frances made their way, early that evening, to the guest-house of Shona MacLeod. This was the first time they had actually met Shona and they naturally offered their condolences. These were received with quiet courtesy, after which the brave landlady took them into the spacious kitchen and offered the travellers tea and warm home-baked scones. There sat their good friend the Reverend Donald Angus MacLeod who rose and extended his hand.

"I'm glad you could both make it. Once we have had a bite to eat, we can walk to the church. It's not far."

The 'bite' was a generous repast. To complement the scones, butter, cream and a range of home-made jams were on offer, of which Richard made a good account.

With a mock scowl, Frances rebuked her beloved in an exaggerated Irish accent, "Tuck in why don't you? You'll end up fatter than a Drogheda pig."

Spraying crumbs Richard retorted, "I'm just doing justice to Shona's excellent scones. I wouldn't want to hurt Shona's feelings by having just one. These scones are even better than my aunt's in Brixham and she made a powerful good scone."

Shona laughed, for the first time since news of her husband's death. She rather liked this unlikely Donegal ex-nurse and Devonian ex-monk.

"Well, thank you Richard. I'm flattered and we have time enough before the service starts."

With that the doorbell rang. Inspector MacGillivray and Sergeant Nicolson were ushered into the kitchen and offered a share of the refreshments at hand.

"Thank you, no, Mrs MacLeod, and we're sorry to bother you on a Sunday, but I understand that Richard Wells is here."

"Yes that's me", responded the ex-monk. "How can I help?"

"Ah, yes Mr. Wells, we just wanted an account of a conversation you had with a – let me see", referring to his notebook, "em, yes, with a Councillor MacPhedran a few days ago about the late Councillor MacLeod".

Brother Richard related the circumstance and content of the said conversation to the inspector in as much detail as he could recall, which was little more than the Reverend Donald Angus MacLeod had already conveyed.

The inspector frowned, "And that's it? You can't throw any more light on Councillor MacLeod's movements or state of mind?"

"I'm afraid not. At that time, I didn't even know who Councillor MacLeod was or that he was the brother of our friend the Reverend Donald Angus. It was just a chance exchange with a stranger whilst on a ferry crossing."

The police had no further questions and departed, leaving the impression that they were somewhat disappointed that they had not uncovered some fresh clue to progress their investigations.

Shona Macleod, pointing to the kitchen clock urged: "I think you'd better swill that last scone down with a mouthful of tea and head for the church if you want to catch the service."

And so Richard, Frances, Shona and Donald Angus rose, donned waterproofs and joined the trickle of worshippers making their way to Broadford Parish Church. The building was a relatively plain and modest affair with round headed windows, a pediment bellcote and a flat Tudor door-piece. As they followed the other worshippers inside Donald explained that it had been built between 1839 and 1841 to replace the 16th century church of Cill Chriosd.

The ensuing service, which was in Gaelic as anticipated, was quite unlike anything Richard or Frances had experienced previously. The order of service was admittedly broadly similar to other Church of Scotland services they had attended, but what was so very different was the music. Each psalm line was 'put out' by the precentor or leader. The congregation then joined in gradually and slowly singing the words of that line, but at varying speeds with fluctuating ornamentation, thereby creating extraordinary continuous waves of sound that caused the hairs on the back of Richard's neck to bristle.

Donald Angus gave a short and moving tribute to his deceased brother, pending an announcement of a funeral date. Tears rolled down Shona's cheeks in her first display of grief as she remembered the happy times when her husband had been less dissolute. The service was rounded off by a prayer and the 23rd Psalm.

As the congregation exited the church, the minister, the Reverend Farquhar MacPhee, stood at the vestibule to greet his flock with a word here and an enquiry there. He shook Donald Angus's hand solemnly and thanked him for his contribution to the proceedings. Donald then introduced Richard and Frances, explaining that they were friends from the far south of Scotland, but attending a course at the Gaelic college.

In response, the divine pressed their hands and with a grave smile uttered the words: *"Fàilte oiribh dhan Eilean. Tha mi an dochas, gum bi taitneach bhur àm seo"*.[8]

The visiting pair smiled and agreed that indeed they were enjoying themselves, apart", they added tactfully, "from the sad news about Councillor MacLeod".

---

[8] A welcome on you to the island. I hope your time here will be pleasant.

The minister acknowledged this response with a weighty nod and then turned his attention to others who were queuing up to exchange words.

Before the quartet had made more than a few steps in the direction of Shona's house, some others of the congregation stopped them to offer condolences to Shona and Donald and then to offer words of welcome to Richard and Frances.

One of these, Lachie Mackinnon, who owned the small creel-boat *Mairi Bhan* seemed to be anxious to extend the exchange. His words, addressed mainly to Donald, were in Gaelic, but they may be translated thus:

"You know how Ewan Allan was always on about power from the tides and how he wanted the community to benefit rather than some fancy foreigners. Well, I was out with my boat in Loch Alsh the day Ewan Allan died. There were a few ships in the area. There was *Whiteman Pioneer*, which they say is involved with this business of harvesting the tides. One of the other boats was a big Norwegian yacht *Ravnsvart*. I didn't think anything about that until I picked up my cousin Alasdair yesterday from Inverness. He works off-shore in the Norwegian sector and was just coming home to Portree on leave. I told him about what I saw that day. The strange thing is he told me that *Ravnsvart* is quite well known in Norway. She belongs to a Norwegian oil tycoon who is also into power from the tides. It seems to me strange that two ships with different foreign owners involved in the tides were in the area at the time of Ewan Allan's death. But the other thing was; there was a RIB dashing about. It passed quite close to my *Mairi Bhan* and seemed to be heading for *Whiteman Pioneer*, although I can't be certain of that. The more I ponder it, I think your Ewan Allan was on it.

Maybe I'm imagining it, and I thought nothing of it at the time, but that man was wearing a dark suit and – well he looked like your brother. I can't get it out of my mind. I couldn't sleep last night."

"Funny", pondered Brother Richard, after Lachie had left the group to head for his home, "Now that I think about it; remember, when we were at Eilean Donan Castle, we saw a man in a dark suit boarding a RIB and heading off towards Loch Alsh. I wonder if that was Ewan Allan. Maybe I should have mentioned that to the police."

THE PRESENTATION

THE last session of the course at the Sabhal Mòr took place on the morning of the following day, it being Monday. The topic had been the music of the Gaelic speaking people and as a finale the group learnt and sang *Soraidh leis an Ait*, composed by the renowned Gaelic bardess, Mairi Mhòr nan Oran, about her heartache in leaving Skye. A second rendition of the song after lunch produced many a tear, as the company exchanged hugs and took their mutual farewells.

That afternoon, Richard and Frances made their way back to Broadford, where it had been agreed that they would stay with Shona for a few days as paying guests. Frances had been feeling tired and wanted to take it easy after the mental exertions of the course, besides which she felt Shona was a kindred spirit, who could perhaps do with a bit of female support.

Donald Angus was of course also staying by way of familial support, at least until after the funeral, the date of which had not yet been set. It was he who mentioned that there was to be a meeting that night at Broadford Village Hall at which one of the proposed tidal power developers was to make a presentation to the community. He added:

"I intend to go along. How about you? You never know, we might learn something about Ewan Allan's concerns."

Frances demurred, "I'll give it a miss and stay here with Shona, but why don't you go along Richard?

And so it was that Richard and the Rev found themselves that evening in Broadford Village Hall in the company of a large and disparate crowd from the local area and further afield. Donald Angus, of course, knew a large percentage of those present and even Richard recognized some familiar faces from the college, including Einar Lund, to whom he waved, and some from the church service. As he looked around he also noted the large taciturn sailor from the Norwegian yacht *Ravnsvart* taking a seat near the back of the room. Then Lachie Mackinnon spotted Donald Angus and Richard and came over to sit beside them, whereupon Richard mentioned his sighting of what may have been Ewan Allan being shipped off on the RIB on that fateful day of his death.

Before they could elaborate further on the matter, the general hubbub in the hall subsided and the meeting was called to order by Councillor Montague Smyth, one of the other Skye members, who was now fulfilling the role that Ewan Allan would normally have undertaken. Councillor Smyth, or Monty, as he was popularly labelled, a retired chartered accountant from Surrey, had moved to Skye some ten years earlier on being made redundant and had, to the surprise of many, been elected to the council. With his plummy, if somewhat hesitant speech and rather superior attitude, he had little understanding of traditional Highland values, but was regarded as well-meaning and independent of the many competing local factions.

Dinging a water glass with a pen, he commenced proceedings:

"Ladies and gentlemen, may I, on behalf of the council, welcome you to this public meeting at which a presentation will be – em – presented on the topic of – em – tidal power by – em – representatives of Whitelite Power. May I introduce –em – Ms Eva Tillotson – em – Corporate Affairs Director and – em – Mr Franklin

Hendrix – em – Development Executive of – em – Whitelite Power."

The two personages alluded to moved forward on the stage, she in a tight fitting white evening dress relieved only by a large silver brooch featuring the Whitelite sunburst logo and he in a silver mohair suit, white shirt and silver grey tie again emblazoned with the sunburst logo. The contrast with the casual and work attire of most of the assembled audience could hardly have been starker.

The visiting representatives were received in silence, for Highlanders tend to be inherently wary of being patronized by bling.

Addressing the audience with a pronounced Southern drawl, Ms Tillotson began:

"Well, I'd like to thank y'all for coming along tonight to hear what we've got to say about tidal stream energy. I just *know* you good folks'll find it *real* interesting, because we sure do. And let me say that your beautiful Isle of Skye here has great potential for generating this green power that'll make our wonderful planet a better place. Now there's no one knows more about tidal stream than our development director, Franklin G Hendrix, so I'm going ask him to tell y'all about it. Take it away Franklin."

The lights dimmed and the sunburst logo of the Whitelite organization was beamed onto the screen, to be followed by a series of slides and animations.

In the course of this presentation Franklin described and illustrated the practicalities of harnessing, by means of sub-sea turbines, the immense power of the strong tidal currents to be found at several locations round the Scottish coasts. It was undoubtedly a slick performance that ended with the claim that electricity generated by tidal power could not only supply all of Scotland's future needs, but create huge surpluses for export.

As the lights came back on, Ms Tillotson invited questions.

Councillor Smyth resumed the chair and started the question session.

"Thank you Ms Tillotson and Mr Hendrix. Most interesting. Em – perhaps I should say that no licences have as yet been awarded for installation of tidal arrays, but – em – in the event that your company were successful in securing such a licence for the waters adjacent to Skye, what benefits might accrue to our community?"

Franklin Hendrix was quick to respond.

"Firstly let me say that we at Whitelite Power are confident that we will secure a licence. Our technology is world class and our financial backers fully committed. As for benefits to the people of Skye? Simple – well paid jobs over a period of ten or more years."

A murmur of approval sounded round the room, followed by a few questions on some technicalities, for several members in the audience were experienced in the off shore oil industry.

Then from the back of the room an American voice was heard. It came from Chuck McColl, who had attended the course at the Sabhal Mòr.

"Mr. Hendrix, you made a fine presentation. Very impressive, but back home in the US, in Wilmington, Whitelite Power's reputation aint so lilywhite. According to media reports, your company has been found guilty of serious safety violations, irreparable environmental damage has been caused to coastal ecosystems and one of your directors has been charged with attempted bribery of federal officials. I'd advise Skye folks to be very careful in their dealings with Whitelite Power."

The mood of the room was transformed. Who was this American? Was there something in what he said?

Eva Tillotson rose to the challenge with a slightly mocking smile and a soft surgery voice.

"You know what, whoever you are, these smears are unfounded and nothing new to us. Our competitors know we're *way* ahead of the game and have been trying all sorts of dirty tricks to undermine our solid achievements. I can assure the folks of this beautiful island here that Whitelite Power is an honourable entity."

As the audience was weighing up the pros and cons of the exchange, Lachie Mackinnon rose to his feet.

"Mrs Tillotson, I am a fisherman and I fish in the same waters as your company. I have watched your operations from my boat with interest. Last Thursday was especially interesting. A RIB, which I understand belongs to your company passed by me at speed, heading it seems towards your research ship *Whiteman Pioneer*. On board was a gentleman, dressed in a dark business suit, who I believe was our late Councillor Ewan Allan MacLeod and who was not long afterwards found murdered on the foreshore at Camas Cross. Can you explain that?"

A collective gasp filled the room. Lachie was a highly respected member of the community, not given to dramatic gestures.

The two Whitelite executives appeared controlled, but their lightness of touch had gone. They conferred, one with the other and it was Eva Tillotson who again spoke.

"Sir – Councillor Smyth told us about the sad death of Councillor MacLeod earlier this evening. A most distressing occurance. Let me say that Whitelite Power's deepest sympathies go out to his family. I know nothing about the movements of *our* vessels that day, but no doubt there were many others in the area. We will of course look into the matter, but I'm sure you will find that Whitelite Power was going about its lawful business."

The hall buzzed with uncertain whispers.

Richard then felt compelled to rise to his feet.

"Perhaps I can add some further background to this vexed issue. On the day of Councillor MacLeod's death, I observed, on the shore near Eilean Donan Castle, a man in a dark suit board a RIB that then headed for Loch Alsh. I was told by a local man that the RIB belonged to a firm engaged in tidal stream energy development. I suggest that further investigation of this matter should be undertaken by the police rather than at a public meeting."

By this stage in the proceedings Councillor Smyth, as chairman of the meeting, was becoming alarmed at the turn of events.

"This meeting was called to – em – consider the – em – potential of tidal energy, not – em – to discuss the sad death of my colleague, Councillor MacLeod. As the last contributor rightly said – em – *that* is a matter for the police.

If there are no further questions – em – please put your hands together to show your appreciation for the presentation by the representatives of – em – Whitelite Power."

A hesitant and muted applause followed.

A CLOSE SHAVE

A T Shona MacLeod's guest house the following morning, the talk at the rather late breakfast table was dominated by the previous evening's extraordinary presentation in Broadford Village Hall.

Richard had already told Frances about what had transpired before they had gone to bed the previous night, but couldn't resist going over the whole thing again with Donald Angus.

"I have to say, it started as such a polished performance."

"Too polished," Donald Angus interjected, "We Highlanders and Islanders can be a bit suspicious of overly flashy people, especially if they are trying to persuade us to do something. I don't doubt it goes back to the time when the rich fashionable landowners and their factors "persuaded" our people to leave our native ancestral land by burning down our houses.

Anyway, it seems those smooth operators from Whitelite Power left the meeting with their gas at a peep."

"Gas at a peep? What do you mean?"

"Oh, a Scots expression," explained the Rev, "somewhat deflated."

Richard laughed. "Yes, I'd say so. Chuck McColl fairly stuck the boot in, and him such a quiet fellow during the course at the Sabhal Mòr. And yet the Tillotson woman was pretty successful in brushing his comments aside. Then Lachie's intervention really seemed to get them worried, although they tried not to show it."

"But it was your contribution Richard, that put the tin lid on it. The pair of them, Tillotson and Hendrix, were furious. If looks could kill . . .

And by that stage I could see poor Councillor Smyth squirming with embarrassment and desperate to bring the whole thing to a conclusion."

Frances listened with interest to this recollection of events.

"Well, while you boys were having your fun last night, Shona and I had a good heart to heart. I have suggested that once the funeral is over and things settle down, she should shut up shop and come down to stay with us at Dalmannoch for a week or two. The tourist season is now well past its peak."

"Good idea, Francie."

"Indeed it is," added Donald Angus, "And it would give Shona a chance to spend some time with Jessie and the kids".

No one seemed to be in much of a hurry to move and the conversation strayed on to other topics for a time until Richard felt the need to stretch his legs.

"How about it Francie? Donald Angus?"

"Och I'm quite content, love. I think I'll just slob out here." She was in truth feeling queasy and welcomed the opportunity to go for a nap.

The Rev was more disposed to the suggestion, "Aye, why not? I could do with getting the blood circulating myself."

The two men donned outdoor attire and as they were about to depart, Frances added, "Oh Richard, on your way back, if you're passing the co-op, could you pick up some flowers for Shona?"

"Sure thing love. We'll do that and we'll be back in time for lunch."

Donald Angus was of course on his native heath, so he led the way. Knowing Richard's maritime interests, he suggested:

"How about we wander down to the Corry Pier and see if there is anything going on? I used to fish off the end of it when I was a boy."

And so it was that the pair proceeded along the main road, until turning off and over the footbridge across the mouth of the Broadford River. There they picked up the footpath that skirts the shore. The weather had improved compared with the previous couple of days of drizzle. Now the salty air was clear and the views over Broadford Bay lifted the spirits of both men. Striding out, they soon reached the old stone pier.

"In my grandfather's time," Donald Angus revealed, "before the Second World War, the Portree mail steamer used to call here every morning and evening. In those days, the pier had a timber extension leading into deeper water. That has long gone, but smaller vessels still use this stone part of the pier."

After admiring the prospect from the end of the pier, Donald Angus suggested going a bit further along the coast. Thus they made their way past a derelict coach-house and the entrance to the elegant Georgian Corry Lodge, which Donald Angus explained had originally been built as the seat of the Mackinnons of Corry. Continuing along a grassy shoreline path, they came to a rocky headland, which Donald Angus called Rubh' an Eireannaich or Irishman's Point.

As they scanned the seaward view, a fishing boat came into view as it passed between the low lying island of Pabay and the main island of Skye.

"Hello?" exclaimed Donald Angus, "That's the *Mairi Bhan*, Lachie Mackinnon's creel boat. He seems to be heading this way. Let's go back to the pier and find out what the crack is."

Which is what they did.

On passing the old coach-house, Richard thought he caught a brief glimpse of a figure moving within; perhaps, he pondered, someone interested in restoring the dilapidated structure.

As the *Mairi Bhan* approached the pier, the engine's drone changed to a sputter as Lachie put her into neutral and with a quick astern burst the creel boat was neatly alongside. Lachie heaved a line which Richard caught and made fast.

Greeting the mariner as he clambered ashore, Donald Angus held out his hand, "Well, *a' bhalaich*, what brings you into Broadford?"

"Funny thing", answered Lachie, nodding also to Richard, whom he recognized from the meeting after the church service and the presentation, "I got a phone call first thing this morning from some English guy, that he had a dozen creels, almost new and available cheap for a quick sale. He said I was to meet him here between eleven and twelve. A bit out-of-the-blue, but seemed too good an opportunity to miss, if it's an honest proposition."

There being no sign of the English salesman, Richard expressed interest in the *Mairi Bhan*, revealing that he too had been a fisherman out of Brixham some years before. In response to this, Lachie invited the walkers aboard and after a thorough run through of the vessel's characteristics and Lachie's fishing techniques, the three of them yarned for a while on matters nautical. Then Richard, remembering Frances' request for flowers, hastened an end to these reveries and with his companion clambered ashore.

As they were about to head back to the shore path, Lachie called after them:

"By the way, I meant to contact the police this morning about seeing Ewan Allan, but the creels business got in the way. I'll do it when I'm back home this evening."

"Perhaps you could tell them about my sighting too," retorted Richard. "We're staying at Shona Macleod's place if they need me."

"Sure thing Richard. Cheerio."

Once back on the main road, Donald Angus went straight back to Shona's, while Richard headed for the co-op to buy flowers. As he entered he again noticed, loading a large trolley of groceries at one of the check outs, the same sailor from the Norwegian yacht who had attended the previous night's presentation. There was a faint unsmiling glimmer of recognition on the part of the Norwegian, after which he carried on with his loading.

Richard went into the body of the supermarket, selected as pretty a bunch as he could find and made his purchase. He had one more task, which was to get some cash from the ATM at the Bank of Scotland across the road. Starting to cross the road, he was grabbed by a passerby who pulled him back, saving him thereby from being knocked down by a speeding car.

"Whew!" exclaimed the passerby. "That was a close shave. That lunatic drove straight at you. Must have been pissed. Are you all right?"

A SECOND MURDER

ON returning to Shona's guest house, Richard decided not to mention the near miss episode. He did not want to alarm Frances unduly, but in truth, he had got quite a fright. As he thought about it, he pondered – was the incident merely a case of dangerous driving, or more worryingly was it a deliberate hit-and-run attempt?

Lunch was a simple affair – homemade Scotch broth, bread rolls and butter – and no less welcome for its simplicity after the late and hearty breakfast consumed earlier. Frances, however, complained of nausea and announced that she proposed to go to bed for an afternoon nap. Although not in the habit of sleeping in daytime, Richard decided to follow suit.

"I think I'll join you. Maybe a cuddle will make you feel better."

"I do believe it will, my darling monk."

In bed a cuddle was duly administered and a tickle elicited some giggles until Frances closed her eyes and fell into a slumber. Then the shock of the pre-lunch episode brought on an acute tiredness in Richard and he too fell into a deep sleep.

It was about five o'clock when Richard awoke. Frances had been up and about for some time, but she sat on the bedside chair reading one of the magazines piled under the bedside table, until he roused.

"Oh my, I've never known you to sleep like that in the afternoon, you must have been needing it."

Rubbing his eyes as he came too, Richard yawned and admitted that he must have been. He still did not want to mention the incident with the speeding car and ventured:

"What do you fancy doing tomorrow? How about a run in the car to Portree and round the north of the island."

"That sounds nice. Let's see how I feel."

And so the pair relaxed in their room reading, she reading the Scottish Field and he the Fishing News, occasionally exchanging snippets of interest until the dinner gong sounded.

They had almost finished dinner when the phone rang. Shona went to the next room, her office, to pick up the call and after the preliminaries was overheard to say, "*O mo chreach*! How awful. How did it happen? . . ."

When she returned to the company she reported what she had been told.

"That was Hettie Henderson. She has just heard that Lachie Mackinnon has been found dead in his boat. She doesn't know how it happened, but she said the police have been called."

Richard and Donald Angus exchanged dumfounded looks. It was Donald Angus who spoke first.

"But we were speaking to him only this morning at the Corry Pier and he was hale and hearty. Oh my, this is as strange as it is tragic."

"Who's Lachie?" enquired Frances.

"Oh," exclaimed Shona, "he's a fisherman. Lives over at Kyleakin and keeps his boat at Kyle. Very well respected. Mairi, his wife, will be devastated. Mairi Macdonald, she was at school with me. Oh dear, what a tragedy."

As these exchanges took place, Richard's mind was turning over dark thoughts. He gave voice to them.

"There's something seriously amiss here. Lachie was in good spirits when we saw him. But then he said he was going to report to the police the business of his thinking he saw Councillor MacLeod on a RIB not long before he was . . . And he said he would pass on my own sighting to them too. And – another thing – well, I was nearly run down on the road outside the co-op. I think there may be foul play afoot."

Frances was startled.

"What do you mean, you were nearly run down?"

"Well, I didn't want to say, but a car just missed me as I was crossing the road to go to the bank. It would have hit me if a quick witted man hadn't pulled me back."

"Oh my darling; was it deliberate? Oh you're scaring me."

"I don't know. I don't know. It might have been, or maybe not, but it's time I phoned the police. Can I use the phone Shona?"

"Yes of course Richard, I'll get you the number."

Richard got through to the desk sergeant and tried to explain his concerns and desire to provide a statement with regard to Councillor MacLeod and Lachie Mackinnon.

About an hour later, Inspector MacGillivray and Sergeant Nicolson arrived at the guest house door. Shona ushered them in.

The inspector announced. "We have had a message that Mr Richard Wells wishes to make a statement to us. If we could speak with him in private please."

Shona took them to the TV lounge, which was otherwise empty and then signalled to Richard that that was where the police wished to interview him.

Richard entered the TV lounge.

"Ah Mr Wells, we meet again," the inspector began, "please take a seat. You phoned earlier this evening to say you wished to make a statement about the deaths of Councillor Macleod and Mr Lachlann Mackinnon."

"Yes indeed. Let me try to explain . . ."

Richard then described how, after the church service, Lachie had described seeing what he thought was Councillor Ewan Allan MacLeod on a RIB, how that had jogged Richard's own memory about seeing a figure in a dark suit boarding a RIB opposite Eilean Donan Castle, how these matters were raised at the Whitelite Power presentation on the following evening. He went on to report that he and the Reverend Donald Angus, Councillor MacLeod's brother, had met Lachie late that morning at the Corry Pier, at which place he was to negotiate purchase of creels (lobster pots as Richard called them) following a phone call. Then he related the near miss on the road by the co-op. In the end, he explained that the tragic news of Lachie's death had prompted him to contact the police.

"Hmm, let me get this straight." The inspector stroked his chin and looked at the sergeant. "So you're telling me that you and Lachlann Mackinnon both saw Councillor MacLeod in a RIB on the day he died."

"Well no, I can't say whether or not *I* saw Councillor MacLeod. I saw a man that may have been him boarding a RIB and thought nothing of it at the time. Lachie, however, was fairly convinced that it was Councillor MacLeod and was under the impression that the RIB, assuming it was the same one, was heading for a research ship, em, let me think - the *White* something –

the *Whiteman Pioneer*. That was what Lachie told Donald Angus in my presence."

The inspector asked: "And the Reverend MacLeod can confirm this conversation?"

"Yes. He's in the next room, why don't you ask him?"

And so Donald Angus was summoned, and he was indeed able to confirm Richard's account of events. He confirmed that he had been present at the conversation after the church service and also the acrimonious exchange at the Whitelite presentation and mentioned that he had observed that the Whitelite representatives had seemed quite uncomfortable. He also reported the circumstances of the meeting with Lachie earlier that day.

"Hmm, so you were both together on each of these occasions?"

"Yes", both answered in unison.

"And did Mr Mackinnon give any indication that he may have been in danger?"

"No," the Rev responded. "No, he seemed in good spirits and hoping to get a set of creels at a knock-down price." The Rev paused and then asked, "How did Lachie meet his death?"

The inspector looked at the sergeant and then looked in turn at the Rev and Richard.

"He was found in the sea beside his boat. He had been struck hard on the back of the head, breaking his skull. We are treating this as a case of murder.

"I have to tell you that you were the last known persons to see Lachlann Mackinnon alive. I must ask you both to remain on Skye until we tell you otherwise."

ABDUCTED

THE following morning, Wednesday, saw a further improvement in the weather. The sky was blue, the sun shone and, on this windless autumn day, the temperature was unseasonably mild.

Richard again suggested a drive to the north of the island to see those geological curiosities, the Quirang, the Old Man of Storr and the Kilt Rock. And then there were the traditional Gaelic speaking crofting communities of Staffin and Kilmuir that the Rev had described.

Frances was still suffering from bouts of nausea.

"I don't feel I could do it justice my love. Why don't you go off on your own?"

Richard was in two minds. He was reluctant to leave Frances, but on the other hand did want to explore the magical island on which they found themselves, particularly as it was such a fine day.

"Oh go on, you big softie. It'll do you good. I'll be fine here. I'll maybe take a dander down to the shore later, if I feel like it."

And thus it was decided. Richard would go out for a day's drive. He asked the Rev if he wished to accompany him, but the Rev had other plans connected with future funeral arrangements for his brother, once the body had been released by the police. So it was to be a one man trip.

Frances chuckled: "Be off with ye, and don't get up to any mischief now."

"What? Me? Mischief? The very idea."

Richard winked, gave her a kiss on the lips, picked up the car key and departed in good spirits.

The previous day's near miss with the speeding car meant that Richard had forgotten to withdraw cash from the ATM, so his first port of call was the bank and the cash machine. After making the withdrawal, he drove to Sutherland's garage to check the tire pressures and fill up the Renault with fuel.

Fuelled up, he set off out of Broadford on the A 850 bound for the north of the island. The main tourist season was over, the road was quiet, the sun shone and Richard was full of the joys. As he progressed along the shore of Loch Ainort past Luib, taking in the magnificent views of Marsco's cone and the surrounding hills he noticed, in his mirror, a black panel van that had been behind him for some time apparently looking for an opportunity to overtake. Content to enjoy the drive, Richard was in no hurry and, at a straight stretch of the road, the van duly overtook and sped on ahead.

Richard thought nothing more about this until, a couple of miles after the Raasay ferry terminal at Sconser, he spied the same black van parked on the verge with the back door open and a man in the middle of the road signalling Richard to stop.

Richard accordingly pulled in to the side of the road, stopped behind the van, lowered the side window and enquired:

"What's up? Is there something wrong?"

The man replied, "Can you help us? It's the van."

Richard switched off the engine, leaving the key in place. He got out of the car and was directed to the open back door of the van. A second man appeared, who was in fact the big sailor from *Ravnsvart*, and then, in a split second, a black hood was thrown over Richard's head, he

103

was bodily pushed forward off balance and his arms were firmly held and then tied behind his back.

"Oi! Let me go!" Richard demanded. "What the Devil is this about?"

As he tried to struggle, his legs were held firmly and then tied. A voice, that of the man who had flagged him down, urged:

"It's no good struggling Brother Richard. You'll come to no harm. Our boss has some business with you."

Still struggling and protesting, Richard was dragged fully into the back of the van. The back door was slammed shut. He heard whispered conversation followed by the sound of footsteps. Richard then heard the front doors open and shut. The engine was started and the van was set in motion.

As Richard lay in the back of the van in darkness, rolling on the floor as the vehicle took the bends, dips and humps, all that could be heard was the drone of the engine and the rattle of the van's back door.

He tried to stay calm and fathom out what was going on.

Was this to do with the previous day's attempted hit-and-run, if that's what it was? Was it to do with the murders of Councillor MacLeod and Lachie Mackinnon? If so why was he implicated? More to the point, was he next in line? If so why him? And oh my God, what about Frances? What is she going to do if he, Richard, is killed? What about the baby?

* * *

Back at Broadford, Frances's nausea had eased off by the late morning. It being such a fine sunny day she now felt in the mood to go out for a while for some fresh air.

Shona had gone out to visit her old school friend, Mairi, Lachie's wife, or rather widow, to offer what comfort she could. The reverend Donald Angus had, as planned, gone to Portree to discuss future funeral arrangements with the undertaker there.

Richard would probably not be back till evening. All the more reason for Frances to go for a stroll and clear her mind of all the distressing happenings of the last few days.

With something of a spring in her step, she set off along the main road in the direction of Dunollie and then down by the hotel to the shore. There was a pier with small boats alongside. She wandered to the head of it and took in the view over Broadford Bay, the little island of Pabay and the mainland hills of Wester Ross beyond. The sea was mirror smooth reflecting the panorama and the blue sky to perfection. This, combined with the salty tang of the sea and the mesmeric sound of lapping water, had an intoxicating effect on Frances – so beautiful, so peaceful.

"Gorgeous, isn't it."

So spoke a young woman, who had been attending to one of the boats and was now standing beside Frances.

"Visitor to Skye?"

"Yes, we have just been on a week-end course at the Gaelic college, and are taking a few extra days to enjoy the island. It *is* gorgeous as you say."

"Ah, the Gaelic college, the Sabhal Mòr. I don't speak Gaelic myself – unfortunately. My parents do, but I was brought up in Edinburgh. They thought teaching me Gaelic would hold me back. Now I think *not* speaking

Gaelic is a handicap. I suppose I should make an effort to learn. It opens up so many opportunities these days and it carries so much of our culture and history. Do you know that this is the site where Bonnie Prince Charlie gave the recipe for Drambuie to the Clan Mackinnon as a reward for helping him escape to France?"

Frances admitted that she was unaware of this fact.

The conversation continued for a while and then the young woman departed to continue with her chores.

Frances stayed at the head of the pier for a while and then walked back towards the hotel. She entered and ordered a cappuccino. As she sat contentedly looking through the window out over the bay, she noticed a man in a light coloured suit seated at a table on the opposite side of the room, also drinking a coffee. He seemed to be observing her. Each time she looked at him, however, he looked away and pretended to read his newspaper. After a few minutes, he settled his bill and departed.

Frances found his attention rather odd, but thought little more about it. When she eventually finished her coffee, she paid and strolled back towards Shona's guest house. As she approached, she noticed a white Range Rover with black windows parked outside. Perhaps someone looking for accommodation, she thought. As she came closer, the front passenger door opened and the same man in the light suit half emerged. At the same moment, the Rev's car arrived, scrunched to a halt between Frances and the Range Rover and Donald Angus stepped out to greet her.

With the Rev's arrival the man, who was by this time standing by the open door of the Range Rover, seemed hurriedly to retreat inside the vehicle which then drove off in some haste. Following the episode not long before in the hotel, Frances thought this doubly odd, but she was immediately diverted by the Rev's pronouncement.

"Ah Frances, I hoped I would find you here. I'm just back from Portree and I spotted your Renault parked at the side of the road between Sligeachan and Sconser with the driver's window open. I thought it was a bit funny. Richard said he was going to the north end today. Perhaps he decided to climb Glamaig."

Frances frowned. "That *is* strange. I know Richard was keen to see the north of the island. Climbing mountains is not really his thing. What is he up to? I hope there's nothing amiss."

The Rev did not want to worry Frances unduly and suggested going inside."

"Shona said she has left a cold lunch for us. We might as well do it justice."

During lunch, Frances's mind was turning over what the Rev had said.

"Did you notice the Range Rover that was parked outside when you arrived? A man made as though to come out and then, when you appeared, he seemed to change his mind, went back in the car and drove off. The odd thing is I saw the same man looking at me when I went into the Dunollie Hotel for a coffee. Strange. You're not that scary, even though you are a minister."

The Rev had noticed the Range Rover too, but not the actions of its occupant.

The sea air had been a tonic to Frances, but when lunch was over she was overcome by a great drowsiness. She slipped off to her room for a snooze, a slumber punctuated by niggling dreams of Richard, the sea, murder and white Range Rovers.

When she awoke it was early evening and there was still no word of Richard, and Frances was by this time seriously fearful that something bad had happened. The combination of Richard's report of his near miss the previous day, their car parked unaccountably at the roadside and the strange attentions of the man in the light suit had spooked her.

By this time, Shona had come back from her visit to Mairi Mackinnon and was feeling low having shouldered the burden of a second death. This added to the somber mood all round.

"If only Richard would carry a mobile phone," complained Frances. "Honest to God, he must be the only person left in the civilized world without one. I'm worried something awful has happened to him."

Half an hour later, the doorbell rang. Shona answered and Professor Einar Lund was escorted into the lounge.

"Hello Frances, I'm glad I found you here. It's about Richard . . ."

Frances' heart sank.

THE ILLUMINATI

WHILE Frances was fretting about Richard's whereabouts, Hector Woodrow Douglas was preparing to catch the early evening non-stop Air Canada flight to London Heathrow with an onward connection to Glasgow.

This decision came out of a revelation that was as astonishing as it was unforeseen.

After Hector and James had rummaged through Luigi Cassani's office and house, they still felt that they had not got to the root of the issue at hand. True they had clear evidence that Cassani himself had been sabotaging Woodrow Douglas Logistics to the extent that the firm's survival had been in danger. Clearly some other entity had been driving Cassani. That Whiteman Inc. was involved was probable, but hard evidence that it was there, was circumstantial. The one scintilla of light was the mention of the Illuminati and in particular the paper bearing the motto, *Ad majorem noster gloriam* and the text.

> *The next steps in achieving our global purpose*
>
> *Objective A: Suppress interest rates*
> *Current action: Manipulate the Fed money supply*
>
> *Objective B: Dominate China Pacific logistics*
> *Current action: Capture Woodrow Douglas China traffic*
>
> *Objective C: Control European tidal stream energy*
> *Current action: Sort Torkelsen Ravngen, Scotland.*

The business about the money supply and the Fed, presumably the Federal Reserve, was clearly big league stuff beyond their immediate comprehension. The China Pacific logistics objective was now only too well understood and hopefully thwarted. Their next most practical approach, therefore, seemed to be uncovering as much useful information as possible about the Illuminati, Torkelsen and Ravngen.

By searching the web and other sources, it soon became clear that Torkelsen was the Norwegian owner of Torkoil, a significant oil and gas engineering and supply company, He was also owner of a concern, Ravngen, an outfit that was developing tidal energy, mainly in Scotland. The question was: was Torkelsen in league with the Illuminati or their target?

As for the Illuminati itself, that was more problematic. Various sources revealed that the Illuminati covered several groups, both real and fictitious, that had supposed origins in the Bavarian Illuminati, founded in 1776 with the goals of opposing superstition and religious influence over public life, and abuses of state power, but who were outlawed in 1784. Since then apparently various organizations claimed links to the original Bavarian Illuminati, or other secret societies, which conspired to control world affairs, by placing agents in government and corporations so as to gain political power and influence and to establish a totalitarian "New World Order" led from the United States. And of course, it was noted that such clandestine organizations had featured in many novels, films, television shows, comics and the like.

"Hmm, that's all very well," Hector sighed, "but it doesn't take us much further forward. The question we need answered is; who are the guys behind *this* Illuminati that's trying to destroy our company? You know what?" he continued; "We need to flush them out somehow. I'm going to call a special meeting of the board."

Two days later, Saturday, the special meeting of the five board members was called. These were: Hector, his son James, his daughter Elaine, finance director Pricilla Munro and legal eagle Eustace Blake. As a secret and informal meeting there was no agenda, no minutes were taken and no administrative personnel were present.

Chairing the meeting, Hector summarized the sequence of events concerning the sabotage of the company's operations and reputation, including Cassani's treachery, his death, and the malign influence of Whiteman Inc., which was presented as fact.

Hector continued:

"What has emerged, however, is something more sinister. What we have discovered is that a secret organization called the Illuminati is manipulating the whole thing."

There was a gasp followed by a guffaw of derision from Elaine.

"You can't be serious Dad," she quipped, having seen some of the movies and television shows about the Illuminati. "It's all fiction – and I know Brad would say so too."

"Well, I can assure you that we have incontrovertible evidence that this organization does exist and it is behind our woes. You realize that this is a secret meeting Elaine," Hector soothed, "but in this instance it might be useful for you to sound out your husband discreetly and let me know what he thinks. And James, it might be useful for you to sound out Linda on the same basis."

James was quick to support his father's summary of their findings to date and agreed that he would sound out his wife as suggested.

Pricilla Munro was the next to give voice in the rather formal manner that was her wont:

"I have no knowledge of these Illuminati to whom you refer Hector, but it is quite clear from our cash flow pattern that serious manipulation of our company's trading has been underway, and it seems not unreasonable to attribute it to some hidden hand beyond straightforward commercial rivalry."

While maintaining a poker faced silence during these exchanges, Eustace Blake had been taking it all in until at last he spoke.

"In my business, I guess I come across all types – from rum hombres to the great and the good. As often as not, in my experience, it's these pillars of society that stir the shit. You tell us, Hector that a bunch that call themselves the Illuminati, are behind our company's problems. Well, all I can say is that you are probably spot on. I came across a pile of stuff about the Illuminati when I was sorting through the effects of a deceased client, a high-ranking military man. I guess he was some careless about his security, but among the papers was an Illuminati membership list. It included some mighty powerful people in government, banking, business, the law, religion, entertainment and so on. That was a few years ago, but it was clear that their aims were not in the greater interest of mankind."

Hector was all ears.

"Have you still got these papers?"

"Hell no. They were the property of my deceased client's beneficiaries and in my line of work I see all sorts of unsavoury stuff from the real nutty to the obscene. Besides, I had no reason at the time to think the Illuminati was anything but another secret fraternity, like the Skull and Bones or the Masons or what have you."

"Can you remember any of the names?"

"Yup, some, mostly east coast, but there were a few from the west. Come to think about it, Zac Freedenberg, the president of Whiteman Inc., was on it as were a few others like Clinton McCarthy, president of the Western Universal Bank that our company uses. So Hector, if you're asking me if this Illuminati bunch is behind our troubles, I'd bet my bottom dollar on it."

That was sufficient for Hector and after further brief discussion the board meeting was brought to an end.

Early on the Monday evening, Elaine phoned her father.

"Dad, I spoke with Brad as you said and he has come up with something important, about – you know, what we were talking about at the board meeting. Can he come to see you tonight?"

"Of course honey. I'm not going out."

That evening, Hector led Brad in to his study.

"Elaine says you have something for me?"

"Well, yes I do Sir. She told me about your theory that a group called the Illuminati was behind your company's troubles."

"It's not a theory, Brad. It's a fact."

"I agree Sir. I would have thought the idea inconceivable until I was about to leave the office tonight. Most folk had already gone home, but I had an upset stomach and I was in a cubicle in the rest room – well you know. Then I heard two voices. One was our president, Clinton W McCarthy, who was in Vancouver visiting our branch; the other I didn't recognize, but he was very agitated. He said something along these lines:

'Look Clint, things are getting out of hand. First Cassani gets caught before we could finish off Woodrow Douglas and now I've just had a call from Scotland. Eva – I can't remember the name – is up to high doh. They've just come out of a Whitelite PR presentation on the Isle of Skye and some fisherman, and another guy they call Brother Richard, have said at the presentation that they saw the councillor on our boat just before we bumped him off. I've ordered Whitelite to silence them, before they go to the police.'

"I remembered that you had told us about Brother Richard when you were over in Scotland. I suppose this could be the same Brother Richard and it sounds as though he is in danger. From what I could make out, Clinton McCarthy sounded real worried, saying that the bank had a lot of money riding on Whiteman and Whitelite. Then the other guy said something about Torkelsen sniffing around and that they'd need to deal with him. But then McCarthy said:

'This is potentially disastrous. We need to call an immediate meeting of the Illuminati to sort this out once and for all.'

"That was it Sir. They went out of the rest room. I waited a few minutes until the coast was clear and then phoned Elaine to call you to let you know that I wanted to speak with you."

"Well Brad, thank you. That's some story. It not only confirms our findings, but suggests that we may have

114

an ally across the water. On the basis that my enemy's enemy is my friend, I need to meet this Torkelsen guy. And what's more, if Brother Richard is in trouble, I'll need to get involved."

Then Hector remembered the incriminating business card he had picked up from Luigi Cassani's desk. He went to his safe, opened it and rummaged through the papers they had rescued.

"Ah yes, here it is – Eva Tillotson, Corporate Affairs Director of Whitelite Power Inc., Wilmington, North Carolina. This may come in handy."

ILLUMINATI

SHANGHAIED

PROFESSOR Lund's arrival at Shona's guest house and his mention of Richard made Frances fear the worst. The professor immediately detected her apprehension and sought to allay it.

"It's all right Frances. Richard is safe and well. Don't worry. It's a little bit complicated."

The professor paused to collect his thoughts.

"Richard was in some danger earlier today, but he is now well out of harm's way. Now he wants to make sure of your own safety, Frances, so you are to stay here tonight and then meet him tomorrow well away from Skye. And, by the way, I have brought your car back. It's parked outside."

Frances did not know whether to be pleased that Richard was reported as safe, or much alarmed that he had been in danger, or indeed that she herself was in some kind of peril.

"I don't understand. What sort of danger was Richard in?"

Einar stroked his chin.

"I don't know all the details, but it's to do with Whitelite Power. It seems that Richard has some sort of evidence that points to them – how can I say – that they may have had something to do with the murder of Councillor MacLeod."

Frances was confused. "B-b-but what? – How? Oh my God"

She stopped.

"Einar, this is Shona MacLeod, owner of this guest house and the wife, sorry, widow of Councillor MacLeod."

"Oh, I'm sorry, I didn't realize. Mrs MacLeod, may I offer my sympathy. This must be a bad time for me to be coming into your home. I'm sorry."

Shona shrugged. "It's all right Mr . . ?"

"Professor Einar Lund. Please call me Einar."

"Well Professor – em – Einar. Your being here is the least of our worries. The fact you have let us know that Richard is safe is a relief. Perhaps I should introduce my brother-in-law, my late husband's brother, the Reverend Donald Angus MacLeod."

Einar made a slight bow in the formal style of the older generation of Norwegians. "Reverend MacLeod, please accept my sympathies for your loss too."

After the Rev acknowledged Einar's condolence, there was a slightly embarrassed silence and then Einar spoke again.

"You are also staying here, Reverend MacLeod?"

"Yes indeed; until my brother's funeral."

"I'm glad there is a man in the house, if I may say so. To strengthen – em – our forces. I have been instructed – with your permission Mrs MacLeod – to stay here overnight, just as a precaution."

Shona agreed that this was in order and, to put a more positive gloss on what was becoming a somewhat confusing set of circumstances, she suggested that Einar stay for dinner, an invitation that was graciously accepted. He then retrieved some night things from the car and was shown to his room.

The meal was a hearty one and, notwithstanding the sense of siege, or perhaps because of it, there was much joviality and laughter, even on the part of Professor Lund, whom Frances had hitherto regarded as rather a dry old stick.

At the conclusion of the meal, Einar tinkled his glass.

"Ah hem, Mrs MacLeod; that was an excellent meal. As we say in Norway, *Tak for maten og godt selskap* – thank you for the meal and good company. Now before we head to our rooms for an early night and an early start in the morning, this is the plan . . ."

* * *

It had been difficult for Richard to tell quite how long he lay in the back of that swaying van, thinking dark and perplexing thoughts, but eventually the vehicle seemed to slow, make a couple of sharp turns and stop. The engine was switched off, he heard the sound of the front doors opening and voices, spoken softly in a language he could not recognize.

After perhaps a minute, Richard heard the back door open and hands helped him to sit up with his tethered feet dangling over the tailgate.

A new voice spoke:

"I must apologize for the rough handling Brother Richard, but I'm afraid, in the circumstances, we had no alternative. Your life is in danger and we had to find a way of getting you out of harm's way without your – what is the word? – hunters knowing where you have gone. If you will let me unbind your feet, we will take a few steps and then I can remove the hood and free your arms."

The voice was calm and almost soothing, with a strong accent, rather like that of Professor Einar Lund.

As Richard eased the cramp in his legs and stood up, still hooded, he asked, "Who are you? Where have you taken me?"

"Everything will become clear in a few minutes. Now come this way."

Hands supported Richard as he was led forward.

"A step up here." And then, "a step down here. That's it. Now just give me a minute and I'll be right back to free you."

A few more steps and Richard was guided onto a padded seat. He could hear the sound of water lapping, the cry of gulls and the quiet gentle rumble of engines. He sensed the once familiar slight motion of a deck under him and smelt the shipboard smells of the sea.

Orders were given in that unfamiliar tongue, there were two splashes of bow and stern lines being cast off and the low engine rumble increased in tempo.

"Right, let's get that hood off and your hands untied."

As the hood was lifted, Richard blinked in the bright sunlight and beheld a large, well-built bearded man. He was wearing a patterned Norwegian sweater and skipper's peaked cap.

He wore a sympathetic look and said, "If you will stand up, I'll free your hands."

This done, Richard opened and shut his hands to restore the circulation and, as he looked round, he saw that he was on board a ship that was departing from a pier on which stood the man who had abducted him on the road.

Richard turned again to the figure who had freed him of his bonds and who now held out his hand to shake Richard's still somewhat numb right hand.

"Ragnar Torkelsen at your service." He smiled; "I must apologize again for these strange circumstances under which we meet, but we had to save you from almost certain death. In fact you had a narrow escape yesterday when you were nearly run down by a car. If we hadn't – what can I say – Shanghaied you, it was only a matter of time before they would have tried again."

"Who are 'they'?" Richard asked, completely confused by all that had transpired.

"I will explain shortly, but first let me show you round my ship *Ravnsvart*. I think you will like her."

The tour commenced and Ragnar expounded, "She's 40 metres, twin screw with a top speed of 25 knots, although we generally cruise at 10 to 12 knots. At that speed, it's more comfortable and saves fuel. On the main deck here we have a main saloon or lounge, dining area and full galley."

Richard observed, openmouthed, the restrained, but luxurious furnishings of the saloon with its two large settees, several armchairs and a large coffee table all separated from the dining area whose table could seat ten. On the upper deck Richard took in the sky lounge, cocktail bar and access to the flying bridge or sky deck as Ragnar called it, from which he noted that *Ravnsvart* was steaming down a sheltered loch towards the open sea.

"Loch Dunvegan, in case you were wondering," Ragnar elucidated. "We're heading into the Little Minch. Now let me show you the bridge."

As Richard anticipated, this pilot house was equipped with every conceivable navigational aid. In the pilot seat at the helm, sat a stunningly beautiful blond haired young woman. She turned, smiled and shook Richard's hand with a firm handshake.

"Allow me to introduce the captain, my daughter Liv," declared Ragnar with paternal pride.

"I'm pleased to meet you Brother Richard. Welcome aboard."

Richard responded, "Thank you, and I'm pleased to meet *you*."

With that, the burly sailor that Richard had encountered on a number of previous occasions, most recently in the course of his abduction, appeared on the bridge.

He too held out his hand: "I'm sorry we ill-treated you, but I was under orders to snatch you, before you were taken by the enemy. No hard feelings I hope. I'm Olaf Andersen, bosun, cook and deck swabber."

Richard shook Olaf's outsized hand.

"I must admit, you did take me by surprise, but no hard feelings – I think."

"We have one more crew member, our engineer, Knut Skallestad. He's down in the engine room testing the electrical system just now. You'll meet him later."

Introductions having been made, Ragnar advised, "Now let me show you your quarters. You will be with us for a day or two. Your wife will be informed that you are safe and well."

Richard was shown to a comfortable en-suite stateroom equipped with a double bed.

"Why don't you freshen up and then meet me in the sky lounge. We can have a coffee there, or something stronger, if you wish, and I'll try to explain everything."

When Richard arrived at the sky lounge some fifteen minutes later, Ragnar Torkelsen was standing at the bar operating the coffee machine. He filled a cup for himself.

"Ah there you are. Coffee? Tea? Beer? Whisky? Brandy? What would you like?"

"Oh, coffee would be fine. Milk and no sugar please."

Ragnar prepared another cup.

"It's a fine day. Why don't we sit out on the quarterdeck?"

And with that, the pair took their coffees aft to comfortable chairs. Richard noted that *Ravnsvart* was, by this stage, rounding a headland, Dunvegan Head in fact, and was now heading into the open water of the Little Minch.

R AGNAR paused, as though considering how to start. Then he spoke.

"About a month ago my wife Elspeth died. She was killed — murdered. I loved her very deeply. She was — how can I say — my soul mate. So you will understand my grief. What made it difficult, almost impossible, to bear was that there seemed to be no motive. The police could not make any progress. It is only in the last few days that I have found out who the killer was. What I can say is that a great evil is afoot.

"Elspeth was Scottish. She graduated in engineering from Robert Gordon's in Aberdeen and naturally gravitated to the oil and gas industry. She was talented — very talented — but at first her talents were not well appreciated by her employers. They saw her perhaps as — what's the term — eye candy in the sales department, rather than as a serious engineer. I met Elspeth at an oil and gas exhibition in Stavanger. I liked her immediately. You might say it was love at first sight. I was just starting out with my own company at that time and I offered her a job. It was a risk, of course, but she agreed to jump ship, so to say, and join me.

"Her joining me turned out to be the best thing that ever happened to the company and to me. Those were the oil boom years. Her practical engineering skills and her way with people were such an asset that the enterprise flourished. She not only learnt to speak fluent Norwegian, but when she got the time, she also immersed herself in the lore of the Old Norse Sagas. Her enthusiasm was infectious and after a bit I too got more interested in the old stories and beliefs of our Viking forefathers.

"A year and a half after we met, we married. We worked hard and our company, Torkoil A/S, and our family grew, as first our son Torkel and then our daughter Liv were born. We decided to get away, when we could, from the pressures and distractions of Bergen's business and social scene, by creating our own special fjordside retreat at a place called Ravnstraum. It is of course very commonplace in Norway to have a country *hytte* to escape to at weekends and holidays.

"Then we went through a bad time. There was a gas explosion at our main plant. Three of our employees died. It was put down to a faulty valve and we were accused of negligence. We had in fact been very careful about safety and, although I could never prove it, I believe it was not an accident but sabotage. This incident damaged our reputation and nearly broke the company. Just as we were pulling things together, our son Torkel died. That broke our hearts."

Ragnar paused with a frown and distant look, as though still feeling the pain of these events. He rubbed his eyes and recommenced his narrative.

"*Ja vel*. These tragedies were all too much for us and we decided to move our administration out of Bergen to Ravnstraum. Many people said we hid from the world. Perhaps we did, but Ravnstraum is a special, and I would say an enchanted, place. Gradually our grief eased, especially as our daughter Liv grew and gave us much joy.

"Elspeth and I set to work rebuilding the business. Engineering has always been our main activity, but we diversified into supplying off-shore rigs and production platforms with a second-hand supply ship. We now have a fleet of half a dozen state-of-the-art vessels. So you can believe me when I say, Torkoil has done very well out of the oil and gas industry.

"But the world is moving away from hydrocarbons, towards renewable and sustainable energy. For that reason we have been developing turbines to harness the energy of tidal streams. The beauty of the idea is that mid-water, when the tidal stream is strongest, is at a different time for different coastal locations. So, you see, the tide is always running somewhere. And if the whole thing can be connected up to the grid, there can be a huge more or less constant, reliable and clean power supply available twenty-four hours a day, seven days a week. In all of Europe, Scotland has some of the best potential sites for tapping this kind of energy. So we set up a new company, Ravngen, to do just that, and we have been negotiating with the Scottish authorities to secure sites. Naturally, we are not alone in these ambitions, but our turbine is by far the most efficient.

"Of course Elspeth and I always kept a close watch over the whole operation, but we have been very lucky with our management and research personnel and for the last few years, to a fair extent the oil and gas side of the business has run itself.

"Although tidal stream research and development is now our main focus, we had more time for other interests in the last few years. We always had boats of one kind or another, but a couple of years ago we picked up *Ravnsvart* from an English yard, after the original commissioning client had got into financial problems. She's a Sunseeker 131 and we fitted her out to our own requirements and took time out — a month here and a month there — to explore Scandinavian waters — Norway, Faeroes, Iceland, the Baltic archipelagoes. Next year Elspeth wanted to really get to know the Scottish islands — but — that won't be possible now. Elspeth's death has changed everything."

Ragnar paused. Richard realized that the mention of this heartbreak and the memory it evoked must have shaken the big quiet Norwegian. He stood up, took deep breaths of the strong sea air, and gestured to Richard to follow him up to the flying bridge. There they both observed the evolving scene. To port, *Ravnsvart* had just passed a rocky headland topped by a lighthouse.

"That's Neist Point, the most westerly point on Skye."

To starboard at some distance the horizon was filled by a long line of land, low in parts, but interspersed with high hills.

"The Outer Hebrides," Ragnar explained. "And coming into view ahead of us the Cuillin Hills. Magnificent aren't they? They remind me of Lofoten, back in Norway. And then beyond that the hills of Rum. Very nice – very nice."

Ragnar fell silent again, leaving Richard to absorb the expanse of the island studded Sea of the Hebrides which on that clear sunny autumn day was looking its best.

After a bit, Ragnar suggested another coffee and resumption of their seats on the quarterdeck. His narrative continued.

"It all started with a take-over bid for Ravngen by Whitelite Power Inc. I had no interest in selling out and made that clear. They then tried different tactics to undermine us – negative articles in technical journals by supposed independent experts – one of our key research engineers was beaten up by thugs who were never traced

– attempted sabotage of one of our ships, fortunately discovered before any harm was done – labour unrest, and so on. We couldn't prove anything, but we were sure Whitelite was behind it. Then one night Elspeth went to check up on an electrical fault on our test turbine at Ravnstraum. The turbine is linked to the shore by a gangway. Near the outer end the support for the deck had been almost cut through. It gave way under Elspeth's weight and she fell to her death in the fjord. She had cracked her head in the fall and her body was washed up the following morning."

He paused and added, "You can never imagine my grief."

Taking my best engineer was bad enough, but taking the woman I loved – my soul mate – was too much to bear and for four weeks, I was a broken man. In some ways I still am.

"When I discovered the evil hand that was behind Elspeth's death and my other misfortunes, I vowed to Odin in the presence of our *ting*, or council, to undertake a death moot. In that way I would take my retribution."

Valknot – the knot of the slain

WEST ACROSS THE SEA

T HE habit of the Norwegian Vikings of old was to set out *vest over havet*, west across the sea, to plunder and later colonize new lands. Some took a northern course to Shetland, the Faeroe Islands, Iceland and Greenland. Leif Erikson even reached North America centuries before Columbus. Others took a southerly course to Orkney, round Cape Wrath (the name comes from Old Norse, *Hvarf*, meaning turning) to the Hebrides. These they called *Suðreyjar* or southern isles, as distinct from the northern isles of Orkney and Shetland, all of which were part of a string of Norse territories stretching from Norway to the Isle of Man and Dublin.

It is this southerly course that Ragnar, Liv and their crew took in *Ravnsvart* towards their death moot.

Listening to Ragnar's account, Richard was fascinated and not a little perturbed to hear of the death moot, which was quite at variance with his own Christian principles, although he could well understand the desire, the need even, for revenge.

"But what is the evil hand you speak of? Do you mean Whitelite Power?"

"Well, yes and no. Once I got some kind of self-control back after the shock of Elspeth's death, and Liv was the one who pulled me through, we started our investigations. We already had a spy working in Whitelite's Aberdeen base, Dod Duthie, an old university pal of Elspeth's. He was able to get us the codes into their internal communications. With this access, we were able to view traffic between them and their parent company Whiteman Inc., a big American conglomerate, mainly involved in logistics and servicing the oil and gas industry. Most of this traffic is routine and time-consuming to monitor, but now and again we picked up incriminating material that pointed to them taking steps to damage Ravngen and Torkoil as well as other operators.

"One of my employees, and fellow Odinist, Sigurd Jacobsen, is a little bit autistic, but he's a genius hacker. I put him on the job of digging deeper and he came up with something that blew me away."

Richard could hardly believe this tale of industrial sabotage and Ragnar's counter play of espionage. What next?

Ragnar continued:

"Sigurd discovered and cracked a highly secure link between Whiteman's president and chief executive officer and a secret organization which calls itself the Illuminati. – a kind of super Freemasons. The Illuminati are pulling the strings of Whiteman and in turn Whitelite Power and its purpose is domination of world trade, energy and finance."

Richard was inclined to laugh, but noting Ragnar's demeanor of deadly seriousness, he ventured:

"But surely the Illuminati are fiction, an invention. I've read books and seen the film that features the Illuminati, surely they're not for real.

"Oh, I'm afraid these people who call themselves the Illuminati are only too real and very well-connected, powerful and dangerous. And it's here on the west coast of Scotland that there will be a – how do you say – a showdown between them and us."

"Wow!" Richard was flabbergasted. "This is scary. And how is it that *I'm* caught up in it?"

"Let me say, in a way I'm glad you are, because you have put something of a spanner in Whitelite's works so to say. But let me go back a bit.

"We have an agent in Skye who analyses our measurements of tidal flow and looks after our interests generally. His name is Jimmy Ritchie, another of Elspeth's's old Aberdeen contacts. He's a hydrologist by profession and based at the Gaelic college. He has been keeping us informed about Whitelite's activities in this area and has been liaising with the council, the Scottish Government and other bodies about leasing sea-bed rights, landward site permissions, transmission bye-leaves and those sorts of things. Actually, you met him today; it was Jimmy who stopped you on the road and – em – persuaded you to join us."

"Mm, not the most courteous of men," Richard opined.

"True. Jimmy is an excellent scientist, but not such a good diplomat. He got on the wrong side of one of the key councillors who had an interest in tidal power – Councillor Ewan Allan MacLeod. It seems that the councillor had become quite hostile to our involvement. This was a complication we did not need, so my first priority was to meet with Councillor MacLeod to try to smooth things over.

"We left Bergen last Monday in *Ravnsvart* and I arranged to meet MacLeod last Wednesday evening in Ullapool where he was officiating at an event in – what's its name – ah yes, the Ceilidh Place. I went along myself. It was a musical performance by a Dale Campbell and others – a good venue and good traditional Scottish music. After the event, I invited MacLeod aboard *Ravnsvart* where he explained his concerns that the local community should get maximum long term benefit from any tidal stream development. Jimmy had not the authority to offer this, but I reassured him that we would be more than happy to enter into a profit-sharing partnership with the community. This seemed, not only to satisfy him, but to win him over to the merits of our scheme.

"It was getting late and I explained that I was meeting with Jimmy the following morning in Kyle of Lochalsh. He said that he too had to be in Kyle that morning and, as he had had a drink, I think several drinks, he would not drive home that evening, and would still probably be over the limit the following morning. I told him that he was welcome to come with us in *Ravnsvart*. So we gave him a berth, in the same stateroom that you now have. We left Ullapool very early the next morning and when we arrived at Kyle, Jimmy was waiting for us. After a short exchange, MacLeod and he seemed to be reconciled. MacLeod then left us. He didn't say where he was going, but he hinted that he had arranged a meeting with Whitelite, probably Franklin Hendrix and/or Eva Tillotson. Of course, I can't be sure of that.

"While we took on bunkers at Kyle, Jimmy and I went to the Lochalsh Hotel where we discussed various business matters. When we had finished, I returned to *Ravnsvart* and we cast off and headed down the Sound of Sleat. On the way we passed *Whiteman Pioneer*, one of Whitelite's research ships, which confirmed my suspicions about who MacLeod might be meeting."

Richard listened to all this and added, "Funnily enough we saw *Ravnsvart* at Kyle on Thursday and again later when we had checked in to the tower at the Sabhal

Mòr. In fact I saw you on the flying bridge looking at the college through binoculars."

"Ah ha, and it seems I saw you on the tower. And now Fate has brought us together. I take that as a good omen. The college looks most impressive from the sea, I have heard quite a bit about it from Jimmy. I must pay it a visit sometime.

"But to continue. Apart from checking out and taking on Whitelite, another reason for our trip to Scotland was to check out our stream trials, so we steamed round the south of Skye to the Sound of Barra, where we are measuring tidal flow, and then north to the Sound of Harris for more measurements. We were berthed at Leverburgh, Harris, when a policeman came aboard and informed us that the Skye police wanted to speak to us about the murder of Councillor MacLeod. This was the first we had heard of his death and it came as a shock to us. We set off for Dunvegan first thing on Sunday morning where the police gave us something of – what do they call it? – the third degree. We told them all we knew, more or less what I have just told you – that is, the part from Ullapool onwards. We stayed in Dunvegan until today.

"It was too good an opportunity to miss the Whitelite presentation. I didn't go myself. I would have been recognized, but Olaf and Liv did go and picked up on what Lachie Mackinnon and you said about Councillor MacLeod and the RIB. I can tell you that that must have freaked out Hendrix and Tillotson. So well done. Unfortunately Mackinnon paid the price and you would have too if we hadn't snatched you first. Fortunately Olaf saw the attempted hit-and-run at Broadford. He found out who you were and where you were staying through

Jimmy and a Professor Lund who I gather was a contact of his and yours. You know the rest."

Richard shook his head.

"What a business. What worries me most just now is Frances. She's not quite my wife yet, but, all being well, she will be soon and she's carrying our baby. If it was so easy for your people to find me, it will be just as easy for Whitelite's people to find Frances. We must keep her safe."

Ravnsvart ploughed on southwards into the Sea of the Hebrides.

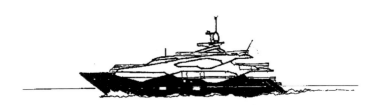

CAT AND MICE

UNDOUBTEDLY Shona had a fuller figure than Frances and her red hair would be a giveaway, but wearing blue jeans more or less like Frances's and a hooded cagoule to cover her figure and hair, an observer from a distance might have been taken in by the disguise. Wearing a long borrowed coat of Councillor MacLeod's and a broad-brimmed hat, also borrowed, Professor Einar Lund accompanied Shona out of her guest house to the driving seat of Frances's yellow Renault Megan. With an unaccustomed flamboyance, he threw a large suitcase into the boot, slammed it closed, moved into the front passenger seat and the car drove off in the direction of Kyle of Lochalsh.

They had not gone far when Shona saw, in the rear view mirror, a white Range Rover, some distance behind.

"Oh, ho. It looks as though that Range Rover Frances told us about is on our trail."

Einar nodded.

"So long as we are in a stream of traffic, they won't dare to try anything. They won't want witnesses."

Fortunately the Renault was in a line of cars, because it was that time in the morning when workers were heading to jobs or meetings in Kyle or further afield. Just after Breakish, they stopped to allow a bus to leave its stop.

"Good," Einar smiled. "Overtake the bus Shona and then just keep in front of him. They won't want a bunch of passengers as spectators."

Then the bus stopped to set down a passenger just before Kyleakin and the Range Rover was soon right on their tail. As they crossed the Skye Bridge, the Range Rover overtook on the approach to Kyle, possibly with the intent to stop the Renault, but if so, the attempt was foiled by the presence of a police car coming towards them in the opposite direction. The Range Rover remained a little ahead of them, but, entering Kyle, as they approached the Plockton road junction, Einar urged:

"Don't signal, but turn off left just here onto the Plockton road."

This Shona did with a squeal of the wheels as she made the tight turn. The range Rover overshot along the main road.

Einar chuckled.

"Well done, we've lost them – for now – but I bet they'll be on our tail again soon. The Rev said the Plockton road is single track, so they won't be able to get past us until we get to Plockton."

And so it transpired. After a few miles, the Range Rover was on their tail again. It tailgated them, flashing headlights and honking. They kept going at a steady moderate pace, if only just to irritate those in the pursuing vehicle.

The Renault turned left past Plockton railway station and into Plockton village, where it stopped opposite the Inn, while the Range Rover overtook and stopped just in front of the Renault.

The front doors of both vehicles opened simultaneously, drivers and passengers emerging. Shona, pushing back the hood of her cagoule to reveal her red hair, flashed a folded wallet containing a medal her late husband had won years before in a darts competition and barked:

"Detective Inspector MacLeod. What the hell do you think you are doing flashing your lights and honking at us." And addressing Einar. "Sergeant; check their vehicle."

"Yes ma'am," responded Einar wearing his most serious expression, which was very serious indeed.

The driver and passenger of the Range Rover were clearly flabbergasted. These were not the dark haired woman and the Brother Richard Wells they had set out to abduct.

Shona again barked:

"Driving license."

The driver, a well-built and nasty looking individual, meekly rummaged in his pocket, pulled out his wallet and extracted his license.

Shona inspected it and then photographed it with her mobile phone.

"Mm – Reginald Pemberton. You are lucky I'm not going to book you for driving without due care and attention."

Turning to the passenger, in slightly less severe tones, she asked:

"Identification Sir?"

The other pulled out an American passport and presented it.

Shona inspected it, photographed the personal information page, returned it and smiled:

"Franklin G Hendrix, I'd advise you to be more careful in the drivers you choose to travel with. Welcome to Scotland."

Pemberton and Hendrix returned to the Range Rover and drove off into the village. Having turned round, they reappeared a few minutes later heading in the direction of Kyle.

Shona was trembling.

"I didn't think I could pull that off, but it seemed to work. Now I need a coffee."

Einar laughed.

"I may be a boring old professor of ethnology and linguistics, but I haven't enjoyed myself so much since I was in the army. I've done the job and look what I photographed on the back seat of their car . . ."

* * *

Some ten minutes after the departure of the Renault, the observer might have seen an elderly woman, in widow's weeds, emerging from Shona's guest house. She was bent almost double, walking gingerly with the aid of a stick and assisted by the arm of the Reverend Donald Angus MacLeod. He helped her into the passenger seat of his Nissan. The minister then placed a couple of bags on the back seat, took the driver's seat, started the engine, selected first gear and drove off in a sedate manner.

"God, I'm dying to take off this bloody hat and veil and coat Donald. Remind me not to grow old."

"Well you can't, Frances. We have to let the decoys carry out their role until we are well clear of the island. Sit back and enjoy the view."

"Hmph. I would if I could see through this veil."

The Nissan turned off right onto the Armadale road and picked up speed. After a while the Rev commented:

"You know Frances, it's not so long ago that this road was single track and really slow. Now we call it the Gaelic motorway. It's so well-aligned, it's hard to stick to the speed limit. Anyway, we're in good time. The ferry leaves at 09:25. And on these straight stretches, looking in the mirror, the road's clear; we don't seem to be being followed."

The drive down the Sleat Peninsula past the Sabhal Mòr and the Clan Donald Centre was accomplished without incident, to arrive at Armadale Pier in time to see the MV *Loch Nevis* berth and discharge a handful of vehicles and foot passengers.

The signal was given for the waiting cars to drive onto the vehicle deck, after which the Rev and the *cailleach*[9] made their way to the saloon. During the passage, over plastic cups of tea they conversed in Gaelic in quiet tones as befitted an old and apparently very pious Highland lady and her minister. Scarcely had they finished their tea, when the half hour crossing was accomplished and the announcement was made that motorists were to rejoin their vehicles and prepare to disembark.

As they drove up the linkspan, Frances noted that the research ship *Whiteman Pioneer* was berthed in the adjacent outer harbour.

"Donald, That's the ship that belongs to the Whitelite people. Let's get out of here before we're seen."

After a few miles they stopped at a layby on a straight stretch of road and waited for five minutes. A

---

[9] Gaelic, pronounced Kalyach, (ch as in loch) meaning old woman

number of cars passed at speed. There was no indication that they were being pursued.

"I think we can dispense with our masquerades now."

Now in more comfortable attire and a more relaxed frame of mind, the Rev and Frances continued southwards. As they progressed, the Rev pointed out interesting landscape features.

"That's the sands of Morar and beyond the isles of Eigg and Rum."

It was another clear sunny day and Frances was entranced by the splendor of the seascape and by the area's historical associations. As they passed Loch nan Uamh, the Rev explained that that was where the Young Pretender, Prince Charles Edward Stuart, Bonnie Prince Charlie first stepped ashore on mainland Britain in July 1745 and from where, in April 1746, he escaped to the Hebrides after the defeat of his forces at the Battle of Culloden and where he finally embarked for France from Scotland in September 1746 never to return.

To keep off the main roads as far as possible, the fugitives turned right at Lochailort to follow the picturesque coastal road by Glenuig and thence through Acharacle and Strontian to Lochaline. Across the water before them lay the Isle of Mull.

"This is the back door to Mull," the Rev explained. "We catch the ferry here for Fishnish. The next ferry is at 12:45, so we have time for a cuppa."

They repaired to the nearby café.

The ferry crossing took about twenty minutes, after which commenced the final leg of their journey to Fionnphort in the far south west of the Ross of Mull, which they reached at just after a quarter past two.

A turquoise sea lay before them. A ferry had just departed, heading for an island which the Reverend Donald John MacLeod proclaimed with pride as:

"*Ì Chaluim Chille*[10], The Isle of Iona, where Saint Columba established his mission to convert the heathen Picts and Scots to Christianity."

Anchored in the sound was a large motor yacht which Frances immediately recognized as *Ravnsvart*.

The Rev made a short call on his mobile and two minutes later a black RIB left *Ravnsvart* to make for the Fionnphort slipway. Standing in the bow was Richard, arms outstretched like Columba himself coming to address the multitude.

Frances ran down the slipway and as the RIB touched, Richard jumped ashore into the arms of his beloved.

---

[10] The Gaelic name for Iona, pronounced Ee <u>Chalim</u> <u>Chee</u>lye (Ch as in loch)

JIMMY RITCHIE

THE Sabhal Mòr Ostaig is generally understood as an esteemed seat of learning that provides courses in business, cultural and other subjects through the medium of Scottish Gaelic. It is, however, much more than that. On the multi-faceted campus, known as Aran Chaluim Chille, a number of cross-fertilizing activities in nurture, research and production are carried out by a number of entities and individuals. One such individual is Jimmy Ritchie.

If it may be wondered how Ragnar Torkelsen was able so quickly to identify the danger in which Richard and Frances were placed and how he was able so effectively to organize their rescue, Jimmy Ritchie was the key.

Jimmy was one of a hard-bitten fishing family from Peterhead in the North East of Scotland. In his youth he made a few trips to sea, but the arduous conditions of work on the deck of a heaving and pitching trawler in atrocious weather, coupled with a propensity to sea-sickness, persuaded him to seek another career. So the study of marine science at Aberdeen beckoned. There, as a student, he became friends with fellow students Elspeth Michie and George Duthie, who everyone knew as Dod. There were of course others whose names are immaterial to this story.

After graduation, Jimmy found work with a variety of operators in the oil and gas industry, fetching up eventually in Norway's oil capital of Stavanger. There, of necessity, he learnt Norwegian and entered a relationship with a Norwegian woman, Anna Eriksen. This situation lasted for some years until, simultaneously and abruptly, job and relationship came to an end. Shortly after that, by chance, while looking for alternative work, he met Elspeth, by then Elspeth Torkelsen, who wangled him a job with the fledgling Ravngen A/S. He spent a further year in Norway, until the company needed an agent to look after its tidal stream energy development interests in Scotland. Jimmy, as a Scotsman and the obvious choice, was offered and accepted the post.

Renting a serviced room in the campus at the Sabhal Mòr, with the support of its community of academics made sense, especially as much of the practical research development work was located in the waters of the Inner and Outer Hebrides. Jimmy's skill and experience was well respected although this was offset to an extent by an abrupt manner. Jimmy called a spade a sodding shovel. That character trait notwithstanding, his mission progressed in a satisfactory manner until, as Jimmy himself put it, "The shit hit the fan".

The troubles started when his boss, Ragnar Torkelsen, signalled that a competitor, Whitelite Power, had been guilty of underhand dealings and that their activities needed to be monitored and reported upon. This monitoring included keeping in touch discreetly with Dod Duthie, who had for some time been working in Whitelite's Aberdeen office. Then there was the unhappy falling out with Councillor Ewan Allan MacLeod which in essence boiled down to a clash between Jimmy's abrasive east coast and MacLeod's subtle and oblique west coast cultures. Fortunately, the meeting with Ragnar and MacLeod on their arrival at Kyle smoothed things over, until, that is, it was overtaken by the councillor's murder.

It was on the following weekend that Eilidh Drummond, in an attempt to make Professor Einar Lund feel at home, introduced him to Norwegian speaker Jimmy Ritchie. As it happened, the pair got on well in a solemn and serious kind of way as suited their personalities.

On Monday, Jimmy was summoned to Dunvegan to drive Liv Torkelsen and Olaf Andersen to Broadford so that the three of them could attend the Whitelite Presentation. Einar had got a lift there separately from one of the staff at the college. During the presentation, when Chuck McColl castigated Whitelite over malpractice and Lachie and Richard made their revelations about the probability of Councillor Macleod being on the Whitelite RIB, the Ravngen group immediately sensed danger. Olaf recognized Richard and Einar from their brief meeting at Kyle. Liv asked who they were. This information Einar was able to furnish regarding Chuck McColl and Richard, but not Lachie who he had not met before. Einar also alluded to Frances, who was not in attendance at the presentation. Jimmy drove Liv and Olaf back to Dunvegan, where they all spent the night on board *Ravnsvart*, having first reported events at the presentation to Ragnar.

On the following morning Jimmy took Olaf back into Broadford Co-op to pick up supplies for *Ravnsvart*'s galley. That is when Olaf observed the hit-and-run attempt on Richard, which was of course reported to Ragnar on return to *Ravnsvart*.

Ragnar was quick to react.

"We must save these people from Whitelite. It's time for us to go on the offensive. Jimmy, find out where the McColl man, the fisherman and this Brother Richard are staying. We must remove them to safety. Keep me informed."

There was more toing and froing for Jimmy, firstly to speak to Einar at the Sabhal Mòr to find out that Chuck McColl had left Skye that morning and that Richard and Frances were staying at Shona MacLeod's guest house. Jimmy then went to check out the guest house's location. By the time he had ascertained Lachie Mckinnon's residence, however, the word was out that he had been killed.

On reporting all this to Ragnar by phone, the plan was formed to abduct Richard the following morning. That plan required Olaf to be picked up at Dunvegan and taken to Broadford. There Olaf had to be ready in the van while Jimmy was to keep a watch on Shona's place until Richard emerged, and thereafter to monitor Richard's movements until the opportunity to abduct him presented itself, as indeed it did on the road just before Sligeachan.

Once Richard was safely delivered to *Ravnsvart*, the plan was devised to get Frances to safety to prevent her being taken as a hostage or worse. To effect this, Jimmy had to drive from Dunvegan to the Sabhal Mòr to try to locate Einar. This took some time. Once located, Einar was briefed as to the situation and urged to make preparations for execution of the plan. This required some technical input which was provided at a unique facility on the campus.

That facility is a fully equipped radio and television studio which is used to train personnel who aspire to work in the Gaelic media. Besides the wealth of electronic gadgetry that is to be found there, there are some rather clever and ingenious people who can work wonders in fabricating specialized equipment. It was a

144

teckie student, Kevin O'Mallie, who was able to create a device to Jimmy's requirements, namely, a miniature microphone linked to a battery powered transmitter – in other words a bug. A receiver and digital recorder were then tuned to the bug's frequency and fitted up in Jimmy's office.

Einar was then taken to where Richard's car had been left at the roadside on the Sligeachan Road, so that he could drive it back to Frances at Shona's guest house, where he was primed to put Frances's mind at ease regarding Richard's safety, and to explain the plan of decoy and escape for Frances in the Reverend Donald Angus MacLeod's car.

On the next morning the plan was put into action, leaving Jimmy to pick up Einar on his return from Plockton and take him back to the Sabhal Mòr. There Jimmy would monitor the bug that had been placed in the white Range Rover. He was amused to hear that Shona had borrowed Einar's Norwegian mobile phone to put in an anonymous call to the police, suggesting that the Range Rover was being driven erratically and that she suspected the driver was drunk.

Between that Monday afternoon and Thursday morning Jimmy had driven no less than 565 miles without once leaving the island.

That is how Brother Richard Wells and Frances McGarrigle came to be reunited on the slipway at Fionnphort.

IONA INTERLUDE

ICHARD and Frances hugged and kissed oblivious to the world around them, until the Reverend Donald Angus Macleod tactfully suggested that it might be a good idea to get Frances and her luggage onto the RIB.

The Rev had intimated his intention to head straight back to Skye, but Richard protested.

"But Donald, you'll come aboard *Ravnsvart* with us too. Ragnar Torkelsen is expecting you."

"Well, I suppose I could spare an hour or two. The last ferry's not till six o'clock."

The Rev was a man of modest material ambitions, but having been a mariner in his younger days he was secretly keen to have a look round this luxury vessel. Thus it was, that with Olaf at the helm, the RIB ferried its three passengers to the sleek motor yacht, on the main deck of which awaited its bearded owner.

"Welcome aboard *Ravnsvart*. And you are the lovely Frances that I have heard so much about over the last twenty four hours. I'm delighted to meet you. And you, Sir, are the Reverend Donald Angus MacLeod, about whom I have also heard good reports. You will be staying with us, I hope. I understand from Richard that you are, like him, also a former seafarer."

The Rev indicated again that he had intended to return to Skye that day, but, as *Ravnsvart* was to remain in the Sound of Iona overnight, he was persuaded to stay until the following day.

"Excellent," beamed Ragnar, "Then Olaf will show you to your quarters, after which we can have a late lunch."

In the short time Richard had been in Ragnar's company he had not known him to be so effusive, revealing an unexpected, but welcome, sunnier side to his character.

It was well after three before Ragnar, Liv and their guests sat down to eat. The conversation was convivial and animated as each told of their adventures over the previous twenty four hours. Richard was fascinated to hear how, after his 'delivery' to *Ravnsvart*, Jimmy Ritchie had driven to the Sabhal Mòr to find Einar Lund, who he had met some days before; how they had retrieved Frances's Renault and how they had hatched their rescue plan. Richard was most concerned, however, that Frances had been in such danger.

"So the decoy must have done the trick then. How did *they* fare. Did they encounter any problems?"

"Well, I don't know," confessed the Rev. "I'd better phone Shona to tell her I won't be back tonight. I'll ask her how they got on."

He made the call on his mobile and the others listened to his responding "wows" and "oh my" and "that's very naughty" and "very interesting".

When the call was over, he related the story of the chase and how Shona and Einar had nonplussed their pursuers by impersonating police officers. He added that while putting the bug in place, Einar had photographed a couple of incriminating pages of documents that were lying on the back of the Range Rover.

In recalling her own journey that day, Frances, now over her nausea, felt weary and opted for a snooze in the comfortable stateroom she was to share with Richard. The Rev, however, was keen to look over *Ravnsvart* and Ragnar was only too happy to act as guide, accompanied

147

by Richard, who had also come to feel a proprietorial pride in the vessel.

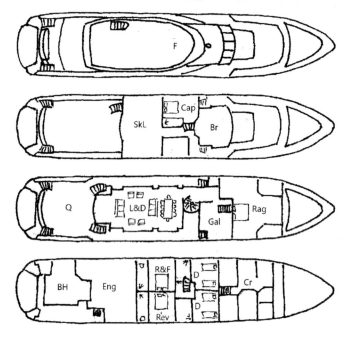

Ravnsvart deck plans showing various locations mentioned

<u>Sun deck</u>: *F = flying bridge*
<u>Bridge deck</u>: *Br = bridge, Cap = captain's cabin,*
SkL = sky lounge
<u>Main deck</u>: *Gal = galley, L&D = saloon and dining area,*
Q = quarterdeck, Rag = Ragnar's master stateroom
<u>Lower deck</u>: *BH = boathouse, Cr = crew's quarters,*
D = double cabins, Eng = engine room, R&F = Richard and
Frances's stateroom, Rev = Rev Donald Angus's stateroom

Olaf meantime went off in the RIB to see if he could catch some fish for supper.

As the RIB sped off southwards towards the open sea, Ragnar declared:

"When we are at sea, we keep the RIB under cover in the boat house in the stern. We also keep a smaller dingy there. I call the RIB *Huginn* and the dingy *Muninn* after Odin's ravens."

Richard and the Rev were of course both practicing Christians, albeit of different denominations, and they displayed some puzzlement as to the significance of the birds just referred to. Realizing their ignorance of Norse mythology, Ragnar explained:

"You see, Odin is the highest of the Norse gods. The medieval Icelandic skald Snorri Sturluson told of how Odin's two ravens, Huginn and Muninn ('thought' and 'memory') would fly off at dawn. When they returned, they sat on Odin's shoulders and whispered in his ears all they had seen and heard."

At this point Ragnar paused and seemed overcome by some misty-eyed reverie. He then commenced reciting an Old Norse verse from Snorri's Edda:

> *Huginn ok Muninn*
> *fljúga hverjan dag*
> *jörmungrund yfir;*
> *óumk ek Hugin,*
> *at hann aftr né komi,*
> *þó sjáumk ek meir of Munin.*

"This describes how Odin cared a great deal about his ravens, so you see, they are very important to us Odinists."

Setting aside his musings, Ragnar resumed his guided tour of the vessel, which took up most of the remainder of the afternoon. Knut was especially pleased to take Richard and the Rev through the complexities of the engine room and the sophisticated electronics that were in truth beyond the understanding of both Richard and the Rev.

In due course, Frances reappeared from her snooze and Olaf returned from his fishing trip with half a dozen codlings he had caught and a bag of langoustines he had bought from a local fisherman.

"Ooo, nothing like fresh caught fish. Why don't I give Olaf a break and I'll prepare the evening meal."

This contribution to the working of the ship was gratefully agreed, especially by Olaf, who led Frances to the very well-equipped galley and then left her to it. When the evening meal was eventually served, the starter was inevitably langoustine and the main course a steaming fish, egg and potato pie, seasoned with herbs, made to a recipe of Frances's aunt from Gweedore in the far west of Ireland.

There was full agreement round the table that the recipe was indeed an excellent one.

The evening was rounded off with what can only be described as a cultural mélange of stories and songs.

All slept soundly that night.

After breakfast the following morning, Richard, Frances, the Rev, Ragnar and Liv were ferried by Olaf in *Huginn* to the holy Isle of Iona. Once they stepped ashore, it was the Rev's turn to act as guide.

"It has been quite a number of years since I was here last on an ecumenical seminar, but it doesn't seem to have changed much. Like many others, I find it a most inspirational place."

The Rev continued:

"It was in 563 AD that Saint Columba, or *Calum Chille* as he is properly known in Gaelic, arrived here from Ireland with twelve followers to found a monastic community. From here he began converting Pagan Scotland and northern England to Christianity. Iona's fame as an outstanding place of learning spread throughout Europe, making it a place of pilgrimage and sanctity, which is still the case today. In fact, forty eight Scottish kings, four Irish and eight Norwegian kings are buried here, or so it is said."

Ragnar was surprised, "Norwegian kings?"

"Oh yes. As you will know Ragnar, the Hebrides were Norwegian possessions for about four centuries and, I can tell you, it wasn't a very good experience for the local population in the early years. It was around the end of the eighth century and the beginning of the next that the Vikings pillaged Iona, butchering the monks and stealing the valuables."

"They were a rough lot," Ragnar admitted.

"Things settled down, especially after the Norwegians adopted Christianity and Iona became a holy place for the Vikings too. Sometime after the Hebrides were ceded to Scotland in 1266, the Abbey Church in Iona became the cathedral of the diocese of the Isles, although for a time it remained under the jurisdiction of the Archdiocese of Nidaros in Norway. Then came the Scottish reformation and the abbey was abandoned and fell into disrepair until just over a hundred years ago. The Duke of Argyll, as superior, transferred ownership of the ruined remains to the Iona Cathedral Trust, which undertook extensive restorations. In 1938, the Reverend George MacLeod founded the ecumenical Iona Community which continues to use the site to this day.

Let's go and see the church."

When they reached the church, each in their own way were moved by the atmosphere of history, simplicity and peace. Frances was struck by the beautifully wrought St Martin's Cross, so reminiscent of similar Celtic crosses in Ireland. On entering the cloister, Richard was reminded of Whitleigh Priory by the Cotswold village of Wethercott St Giles, where he had been a novice until his world changed when moving to Dalmannoch and falling in love with Frances. The Rev thought of the ecumenical seminar in this very church a decade and a half before, where he too had been tempted by an attractive young woman, but that was – well, a long time ago. Ragnar thought of the Norwegian King Magnus Berrføtt. In the course of the current voyage, he had been reading Snorri Sturlasson's *Kongesagaer* (Saga of the Norwegian Kings). This described how the barelegged Magnus 'visited the holy isle and gave quarter and peace to all men there' and that Magnus then wished to open the little *Kolumkillekirken*[11], 'but did not go in and closed the door again and locked it' out of respect for Columba. Ragnar *did* go in to the present building and in atonement for his ancestors' misdeeds decided to make a generous financial contribution to the work of the Iona Community. Since coming to the west of Scotland, Liv had had little opportunity to explore ashore. Here in Iona, she was

---

[11] The Norwegian rendering of Church of Chaluim Chille (Iona), no longer extant

captivated by the island's beauty and timeless sense of history, and vowed to learn more about her mother's Scottish heritage.

A chill in the wind and threatening rain foretold of a change in the weather. The little group returned to the slipway and was taken back by Olaf in *Huginn* to *Ravnsvart*. After thanking his host for his generous hospitality, the Rev was ferried back to Fionnphort to collect his car and make the journey back to Skye.

While Richard and Frances stood by the taffrail waving to the Rev, Ragnar, who had been on the bridge making contact with his base at Ravnstraum, reappeared with a somewhat grave expression.

"Time to weigh anchor. We have to make a rendezvous on the mainland and we've just checked the AIS and *Whiteman Pioneer* has left Mallaig and is heading south."

CORRYVRECKAN

WITH the anchor stowed, *Ravnsvart* headed south out of the Sound of Iona towards open water. She rounded the little islet of Eilean nam Muc that lies to the west of the Isle of Erraid and set out on a south easterly course between the Ross of Mull and the treacherous Torrin Rocks. Once clear of these hazards the course altered to east south east.

On the day of the abduction, Ragnar Torkelsen had quickly ascertained that Richard had formerly been a seafarer. On Ragnar's part this was a welcome development, for *Ravnsvart* had left Bergen short-handed and he was pleased that Richard was more than willing to take his turn at the helm, which he had already done for part of the smooth passage south from Dunvegan.

Once the vessel was in open water, Richard volunteered "Why don't I give you a break Liv and take over for a while?"

Liv was delighted. "She's all yours. Our course is 110. We're heading for Crinan. I'll be back in an hour or so."

With that, Ragnar explained somewhat mysteriously that he hoped to pick up some help at Crinan and then disappeared to his stateroom. The comely blond skipper also departed from the bridge to her adjacent cabin to carry out some administrative chores that are the lot of master mariners, leaving Richard alone at the wheel.

The former monk, former sailor was in his element, in command of a beautiful ship whose sea-kindly hull dipped and rolled gently to the swell, progressing at an economical twelve knots. To the north lay the rugged coastline of the Ross of Mull with the towering peak of Ben More beyond. To the south lay Colonsay, and beyond, the distinctive Paps of Jura dominated the horizon. Ahead lay the mountainous Argyll mainland protected by its string of islands.

Notwithstanding a brief shower and some strengthening of the westerly wind, a pleasant and uneventful hour passed in the warmth of the enclosed bridge. Mull was left behind and ahead lay the rocky and cliff-girt isle of Scarba, rising to almost 1,500 feet, and the equally rocky north end of the very much larger island of Jura. Gradually opening up between them was a narrow sound. It was through this sound that *Ravnsvart* was to ply – the infamous Gulf of Corryvreckan with its treacherous whirlpool.

A few miles before reaching this feature, Liv reappeared on the bridge. She examined the chart and the Admiralty Sailing Directions and after a few minutes declared:

"We are scheduled to be at Crinan in about an hour, so we have to go through the Gulf of Corryvreckan. Listen to what the Sailing Directions say.

When tidal streams set through the Gulf of Corryvreckan, navigation at times is very dangerous and no mariner should attempt passage without local knowledge, nor should passage be attempted with wind against the tide. The passage through the gulf from E to W is more dangerous than a passage in the opposite direction, because the eddies and whirlpools are stronger with the W-going stream. In addition, strong winds from the W create violent turbulence during the W-going stream during which the sea breaks right across the gulf.

"Well we certainly don't have local knowledge. We *are* going from west to east and we have a westerly wind, but as far as I can calculate, we have a falling tide, so the stream is east-going. That is in our favour, but it's near spring tide which means the stream will be at its strongest. I think my father needs to decide whether or not we risk passage through the Gulf. We'll heave-to until I fetch him."

On this instruction, Richard turned the ship's head to windward, then pulled the throttles back to cut the engines to an idle, so that *Ravnsvart* now wallowed in the swell, drifting visibly northwards with the tide.

Liv went below to fetch her father and the pair emerged on the bridge a couple of minutes later.

In silence, Ragnar looked over the chart and the sailing instructions, after which his instruction was clear and to the point.

"We go."

"Richard set our course for Corryvreckan and increase speed to eighteen knots."

"Aye aye sir."

With a happy grin at being trusted with the helm, Richard pushed the throttles forward to half ahead and turned the wheel hard a-port. *Ravnsvart* sprang into life listing steeply to starboard as she turned, and then returned to an even keel when she resumed her course. Richard pushed the throttles further forward and *Ravnsvart* surged headlong towards the dreaded navigational hazard.

At this point, Frances appeared on the bridge.

"What in the name of the Wee Man's going on? We were going along nicely and I was having a nice snooze, then we stopped, then we were lurching about and now we're charging ahead like a bat out of Hell."

"We can go faster than this," quipped Ragnar, "But you are just in time to see the fun."

As *Ravnsvart* approached the entrance to the gulf Olaf joined the group on the bridge, also curious to see what was afoot. Knut, on Ragnar's instructions, was below with his engines to be on the spot in, the hopefully unlikely, case of any malfunction.

With a following wind and swell the motion in the ship had thus far been easy but, suddenly, all on board felt a shock and fierce vibration as *Ravnsvart* felt the effects of the tidal stream and the ship started to spin in a clockwise direction as competing streams grabbed her. In compensation Richard turned the helm a-port, over correcting the course so that the ship now swung anti-clockwise. Another adjustment of the helm brought the ship back on course. Although she was making eighteen knots over the surface of the water, *Ravnsvart* was making twenty five knots over the ground, such was the force of the current. The sea on either side had become very agitated with a lot of chop and white water and the ship seemed to be grabbed this way and that by fierce eddies caused by the action of the strong current over the uneven bottom far below.

"Starboard Richard. We're too close to Scarba and The Hag?"

Richard acknowledged the order and then queried, "The Hag"?

"Yes, according to the sailing directions, The Hag is a very dangerous whirlpool caused by an underwater pinnacle – and look, there it is."

Quite close on the port bow the boiling and roaring whirlpool came into view with huge waves welling up in violent turbulence. The ship was being pulled sideways towards this foaming vortex.

"Hard a-starboard and full ahead. Head for the Jura shore."

Richard complied and the ship immediately surged forward in a violent clockwise turn, her powerful engines sufficient to overcome the pull of that deadly Hag. *Ravnsvart* corkscrewed over towards the Jura shore with white water and spray drenching the wheelhouse windows as Richard alternately spun the helm back and forth until a more settled eastward course could be maintained.

"Well done helmsman, reduce speed to eighteen knots."

Ravnsvart ploughed on past Jura's north extremity of Carraig Mhòr and, after dealing with a few more eddies, passed into smoother waters.

Ragnar, who had kept his cool throughout, gave the command, "Reduce speed to twelve knots and make a course east by south east."

"Aye aye sir."

Richard pulled the throttles back and checked the compass.

"East by south east it is Sir. Speed twelve knots."

Ravnsvart settled to a smoother and more leisurely pace and all on board felt a sense of relief as relative calm descend upon them.

With the pressure off, Richard wiped sweat off his brow.

"Wow! That was quite something. What a ship! She handles like a speed boat."

Ragnar smiled, not a little proud. "I'm glad you like her. And, if I may say so, fine helmsmanship on your part Richard. You can have a job with me any time. Now head between those two little islands. I can't pronounce their names."

Frances, who had been rendered speechless during the passage through the gulf, looked at the chart – "Ah – Rèisa an t-Sruth and Rèisa Mhic Phaidean".

Ragnar was none the wiser, but ten minutes later *Ravnsvart* had passed between these two islets and in a further five minutes or so was passing through another sound, the Dorus Mòr, or big door, between the Argyll mainland at Craignish Point and an islet called Garbh Rèisa. Ahead lay the sheltered haven of Crinan where, after another quarter of an hour, *Ravnsvart* threaded her way through an array of moored yachts and made to berth at a little pier half a cable east of the entrance to the famous Crinan Canal.

There, ready to catch *Ravnsvart's* lines, were three figures – none other than Hector Woodrow Douglas, Holly Garden and John Walker, better known as Whisky.

SHARING STORIES

IT is impossible to say who were the more pleased; the shore party on spying Brother Richard and Frances leaning on *Ravnsvart's* rail, or Richard and Frances taken aback at Hector's, Holly's and Whisky's presence at this out of the way West Highland port.

"Good heavens, what are you lot doing here?" Richard was the first to give voice while Whisky looped *Ravnsvart's* lines over the little pier's wooden stake bollards.

"It's sure good to see that you and Frances are safe and sound."

That was Hector.

Olaf ran out the gangway and Ragnar went ashore. He held out his hand.

"Hector Woodrow Douglas I presume."

"The same. And I presume *you* are Ragnar Torkelsen."

The two men shook hands.

"We have much to discuss."

Ragnar then turned to Whisky.

"*Å ja, Jeg husker deg. John Walker, er det ikke.*"

"*Ja absolutt. Dylded å møte deg igjen, Herr Torkelsen.*[12]

After this exchange of mutual recognition, Whisky then turned to Holly and in English said:

"May I introduce Holly Garden, she has been very supportive of our cause".

"Pleased to meet you Holly. If you are a friend of John Walker, you are my friend too. Now please all come

---

[12] Translation: Ah yes, I remember you. John Walker is it not? Yes indeed. Delighted to meet you again Mr Torkelsen.

aboard. It seems you may already know Brother Richard and Frances."

There followed a melange of hugs and handshakes as old friends greeted each other and as the new arrivals were introduced to Liv, Olaf and Knut.

After allowing time for these courtesies to be observed, Ragnar drew the company to order.

"If I may have your attention. We have serious business ahead of us. Liv will show our new arrivals to their quarters, where you can freshen up and, in say twenty minutes, if you will be good enough, please come to the dining room. Refreshments will be served while we compare notes and make a plan of action."

Olaf then cast off *Ravnsvart* from the pier and Ragnar took her a few cables' length into Loch Crinan and dropped anchor.

"Just in case there are any troublemakers on shore."

While this manoeuvre was being carried out, Hector was put in the double stateroom vacated by the Rev, just opposite that of Richard's and Frances's. Whisky and Holly were given a twin berthed cabin located forward of the doubles. After ablutions, the newcomers joined the ship's company in the dining area where beverages and a cold table had been laid out.

Ragnar sat at the head of the table.

"Please help yourselves to tea, coffee, juice, sandwiches, as you wish and we will start."

After a short pause to allow for pouring of refreshments, Ragnar brought the meeting to order. As English was of course not his first language, he paused to gather his thoughts and words and then commenced.

"We are gathered here because a great evil is at work. It has fallen to some of us – in fact, I believe, all of us here – to fight and destroy this malevolent force. I speak of a secret organisation which calls itself the Illuminati and a corporate entity and its subsidiary which trades as Whiteman Inc. and Whitelite Power. We each come at this from a different – how can I say – angle. It will be helpful if we share what we know so that we can best make our plan of attack. I shall begin by explaining how I came to be here and then I shall ask others to do likewise."

Ragnar then outlined the sequence of events previously described to Brother Richard – his company's developments in tidal stream energy; the undermining of its operations by Whitelite; the murder of his wife Elspeth; the discovery of the Illuminati's role; the decision to take *Ravnsvart* to Scotland for the death moot. He then went on to describe the events of the previous week – Councillor MacLeod's murder; the Whitelite presentation at Broadford and how Lachie Mackinnon and Richard had inferred a link between Whitelite and Councillor MacLeod's death; how this led to Lachie's murder and Richard's and Frances' rescue from danger.

"There is one other important piece of information. The bug that Professor Lund smuggled into the Whitelite Range Rover has come up with something very interesting. Here is a clip from the sound file that my man Jimmy Richie picked up yesterday morning. He emailed it to me."

Ragnar keyed his iPhone and the sound file commenced play over the ship's media system. Firstly the noise of a car engine and then the ring tone of a mobile phone. It was answered by a male voice, that of Franklin Hendrix:

'Eva – well no, we followed her car, but when we stopped it, she wasn't in it. It was driven by the police.'

There was a pause while Eva presumably vented her fury, and then:

'How the Hell was I to know? – The woman police inspector looked like her and, no, she didn't suspect anything. – How should I know where she is? We went back to the guest house, but there was nobody there. – For fuck's sake, if you're so clever, you tell me where they are. It's all getting out of hand. I told you we shouldn't bump off that councillor.'

Another long pause filled only by engine noise and then:

'Yes, I know. I know Torkelsen left Skye yesterday. We didn't get a chance to do anything, but we've been tracking him. His yacht seems to be stopped at some island further south. – I don't know which one. I'll check and let you know. Our best chance to blow him and his yacht up is for us to follow him in the Whiteman Pioneer. There's scuba gear on board. – Yes, yes, I'll pick up the limpet mine in Aberdeen. – Okay, okay, Tomorrow morning in Mallaig. I'll see you on board.'

With a click the recording ceased.

There was a stunned silence as members of the group looked at each other wondering what next.

It was Hector who broke the silence.

"Wow! That was some story. Now we have proof that these lunatics are murderers and we know now what their intentions are. So I guess I should make my pitch which has many similarities with yours Ragnar."

Hector then went on to describe how his own company, Woodrow Douglas Logistics, had almost been ruined by his senior shipping clerk Luigi Cassani, who died mysteriously before he could give evidence; how he and his son James had ascertained that the Whiteman and Whitelite companies had been behind Cassani's sabotage efforts and that behind *them* had been the shadowy Illuminati, among whose aims was to control European tidal stream energy and specifically to 'sort Torkelsen Ravngen, Scotland'.

"So, Ragnar, that is how I first heard of you and, after checking you out, I concluded that we were both targets of Whiteman-Whitelite and the Illuminati. It seemed to me that if we have a common enemy, we would be best forming an alliance to take countermeasures.

"What really worried me was hearing that you, Richard, was also in the firing line and all I can say is, thank the Lord that you, Ragnar, took the initiative to pull Richard and Frances out before they came to grief.

Well, I hopped on a plane to Heathrow with a connecting flight to Glasgow, hired a car and drove to Dalmannoch to see how the land lay. My heart sank as most of the usual suspects weren't there, but fortunately, quite by a lucky chance, I bumped into Holly. At first I didn't know quite what to say, but I thought I'd better just spill the beans and tell her everything, including my concern about Richard and my wish to make contact with you Ragnar. Thank the Lord I did, because she took me to meet John, I mean Whisky, who had been tracking Ragnar's movements on AIS and had indirect contact through his Odinist pals.

"That was yesterday. Through these contacts, Whisky managed to arrange for us to be picked up here at Crinan. As you may imagine I was pretty bushed with the travel, jet lag and general anxiety, so I crashed at my apartment at Dalmannoch.

"Today it was just a matter of driving back to Glasgow with Holly and Whisky to drop off the car and get the 11:58 bus to Lochgilphead where we arrived about half past two. We had a quick snack and a coffee there and then we got a cab to Crinan and here we are."

Hector took his pocket book from inside his jacket and pulled out a business card.

"Ragnar, you mentioned Eva Tillotson's presentation on Skye, and she was clearly at the other end of the phone call you just relayed to us. From what I can gather, she is central to Whitelite's evil plans. This is her business card with her cellphone number. It might come in handy when we go into the attack."

Ragnar smiled a broad smile.

"Hector, I like your style. Attack is exactly the right word. Now that we have reinforcements on board, I think we are ready to go on the offensive."

PLAN OF ACTION

EVERYONE on board the sleek black hulled yacht, late that Friday afternoon, felt a slight judder as *Ravnsvart* lay at anchor in Loch Crinan. The wind had strengthened and the ship was tugging at her anchor so that her bearded owner ordered more cable to be let out to ease the strain. Ragnar then went to the bridge to check the weather report and also the position of *Whiteman Pioneer*.

He returned to the dining room.

"According to AIS, *Whiteman Pioneer* is now at Oban which is only about thirty miles from here. That's two hours steaming time. But I doubt if they'll try anything tonight with darkness falling soon and a severe gale forecast. However, there is no time to waste in planning our countermeasures."

The conference in the ship's dining room recommenced and Ragnar took the lead once more.

"Let us consider what has to be done. As we now know, our enemy is not averse to murder. It is pretty well certain that they killed my wife Elspeth. Then there was, what was his name? Your clerk, Hector?"

"Luigi Cassani."

"*Ja*, Cassani. It seems clear that he was murdered to shut him up. They definitely killed Councillor MacLeod. We have an admission of that from the recording of Hendrix's phone conversation. And then there was the fisherman Mackinnon. That's four murders that we know of. We know they plan to blow up *Ravnsvart* by using a mine. Hendrix's mention of scuba gear points to their method of attack. That is, we can assume, for a diver, or divers, to attach a mine to

Ravnsvart's hull. So Whiteman, Whitelite, the Illuminati, however we call them, are ruthless and dangerous. We should not underestimate them.

"What do we have on our side? It is this. We know their intentions, they do not know ours."

A silence followed, broken by Richard.

"What *are* our intentions?"

Ragnar spoke.

"If I may speak for myself. My intention is to destroy these Illuminati bastards."

There was another, this time rather shocked, silence.

This time Hector spoke.

"Hmm – harsh, Ragnar, but in the circumstances – fair. After all, they tried to destroy us. But how do you propose, in practice, to – em – neutralize Whiteman stroke Whitelite?"

Ragnar pondered for some seconds, then looked into the faces of each of the group.

"We set a trap, with some tasty juicy bait and then – what's the word? – *ja* – entice them to sniff at the bait – then 'snap!' – we have them."

There was another silence and then Richard interposed.

"You say a 'trap', Ragnar, and 'bait'. What exactly do you mean?"

"The 'trap' is to get them to expose themselves for what they are – scheming murderers. The bait is *Ravnsvart* and those on board who are witness to their evil."

Richard then responded: "So if we are the bait and they propose to blow us sky-high with a mine, aren't we putting ourselves in danger to no great advantage?"

Richard looked at Frances, thinking of their unborn child, "I mean there are those on board who are innocent of any connection with Whitelite."

Ragnar nodded slowly and again made eye contact one by one with each individual present.

"Richard, right. *Ja*, you make a very good point. We are – how to say – playing with fire. I will not stand anyone into danger against their wishes and will put ashore anyone who wishes now."

Sensing Richard's apprehension about her safety, Frances broke the silence.

"Look; I know you're worried about me, my love, but we were in real danger while we were on dry land and still would be. Thanks to Ragnar and his friends we escaped death. Sure, we're as safe here as anywhere. And anyway, the sooner we sort out these gobshites the better. I'm for staying on board."

Ragnar clapped his hands in admiration of Frances's colourfully expressed Irish pluck.

Then Holly, who had been silent up to this point, spoke.

"Whisky and I came to help Ragnar in his time of need. We would be dishonouring each of our pagan creeds if we abandoned him now. Whatever our fate, we are here to fight a great evil. Of the noble Odinist virtues that Whisky taught me, it is time for us to embrace the greatest of these and that is courage. With courage and fortitude we can overcome this malevolence!"

"That's the spirit Holly," enjoined Hector, "It seems we are all agreed that we stand and fight. Now Ragnar, where do we go from here?"

"Well, to start with we must let Tillotson and Hendrix know that we have evidence that they murdered

Councillor MacLeod and also suggest that we know of their involvement in the deaths of, what was his name, ah yes Cassani, and Mackinnon. We must also tell the police what we know of Whitelite and their criminal activities and then let them know that we are ready to – how do you say – spill the beans. I think they'll come after us to try to shut us up."

Hector nodded in part agreement: "Okay, so they'll come after us, as you say, and quick, but what then? What are our countermeasures?"

Ragnar made a grim smile.

"I have a few tricks up my sleeve, but more of that later. Firstly I think it's time to ring Jimmy Richie and get him to contact the police in the morning with a message that we have evidence pointing to Whitelite, Tillotson and Hendrix as murderers or accessories to the murder of Councillor MacLeod and others."

Richard added, "The best contact is probably Inspector MacGillivray. While Jimmy Richie is at it, perhaps he should mention that Frances and I are material witnesses".

"Okay, we'll get him to pass that on and get him to mention that we are all together here on *Ravnsvart*. Why don't you come with me to the bridge and we'll make the call from there?"

And so the two men left the assembled company and made their way to the ship's nerve centre. With Richard at his side, ready to prompt as required, a call was put through to Jimmy Richie, Ragnar's factotum on Skye. Careful instructions were conveyed as to what to say to Inspector Macgillivray, essentially alerting him to evidence held by Ragnar and Richard that Eva Tillotson and Franklin G Hendrix, or their agents, had murdered

Councillor MacLeod, Lachie Mackinnon and had made an attempt on the lives of Richard and Frances, which may have been successful had they not been rescued and were now on board *Ravnsvart*, currently anchored at Loch Crinan. This evidence would be conveyed to the police the next day at Oban. Richard added that it would be advisable for Jimmy and the police to monitor the locations of both *Ravnsvart* and *Whiteman Pioneer* on AIS over the ensuing 24 hours, which suggestion was also conveyed to Jimmy.

That job done, Ragnar opened the bridge starboard door to observe the developing weather conditions.

"Good. The sea's rising. That is in our favour."

Ragnar did not say why, nor did Richard ask.

SETTING THE TRAP

REJOINING the others in the dining area, Ragnar related the instructions given to Jimmy Richie. However, the assembled company was more interested to know what the next step was to be. How was the trap to be set?

Ragnar then answered.

"Hector, you mentioned that you had Eva Tillotson's business card with her *mobiltelefon* number. The time has come to give her and Hendrix the shits. The more scared and desperate they are the more mistakes they will make. Time for you to give her a call."

"Okay, Ri-ght, but what do you want me to say?"

"Well, if I understand you Hector, you have never met or spoken to the woman in person?"

"True."

"And you are the only one of us with an American accent."

"Scottish-Canadian. Please."

"Okay, okay, near enough. So I suggest that you phone her as one of the Illuminati and tell her that she and Hendrix have failed in their duty. Her masters are very angry and she must act to put things right immediately. Warn her that we are about to give damning evidence to the police tomorrow and must be stopped. That sort of thing. Do you think you can pull it off?"

"Hmm – a bit of a challenge, but what the Hell? I'll give it a go. Let's just make a few notes first so that I'm as prepared as I can be. Now let me see . . ."

Ragnar rummaged in a drawer and handed Hector a note pad. Hector started jotting down some ideas while others made suggestions as to what to say.

"What if they have secret passwords?" queried Holly.

"Good point. We'll just have to take a chance on that and bluff it," countered Ragnar.

Soon, Hector had taken his preparation as far as he could.

"Right, here goes. I'll put the phone on speaker, and Frances, can you record the conversation on your phone, but for God's sake, not a sound out of any of you."

Hector keyed in Eva's number.

The ring tone sounded – "*dring – dring – dring*" and then a voice.

"*Eva Tillotson.*"

Hector affected a slow somewhat sinister Americanized voice, "Good evening Eva. It *is* evening where you are?"

"*Yes. Who's speaking?*"

"Illuminati business Eva. Illuminati business. You don't need to know. You are already aware that Zac is angry – very angry. I can tell you that Clint McCarthy is incandescent and he is not alone. You have failed us Eva, you and Franklin. You have let us down."

"*But we have done everything we were asked to do. We got rid of MacLeod who was about to back Torkelsen's scheme. We tricked him and got him to come out on the RIB, so Franklin's heavy, Reg Pemberton, throttled him and pushed him overboard. He liquidated Mackinnon too . . .*"

"But the other witness, Brother Richard, is still on the loose. He and his wife are now on Torkelsen's yacht at a place called Crinan. My contact in the law tells me that this Brother Richard and Torkelsen are going to give the police evidence against us tomorrow. They must be stopped. You know the price of failure."

Hector cut the call without waiting for an answer. "Whew. I hope that was all right."

Ragnar grinned, "Perfect. Just perfect."

"Just as well I have a Canadian cell phone. That'll come across as an international call.

Ragnar stretched his arms and then slapped his hand on the table.

"Now for action. First defence. We must be on the look-out for enemy activity, night and day. I have asked our skipper Liv to divide us into three watches. Liv, over to you."

On a flip chart, Liv unveiled a large sheet of paper on which was a list:

Starboard watch: Olaf, Richard and Frances
Middle watch: Ragnar, Whisky and Holly
Port watch: Liv, Knut and Hector

"The officer of the watch is the first name on each line and each watch will do four hours on and eight hours off. There should be at least two on watch at any time and we will start as soon as this briefing is finished. Watches will change at 24:00, 04:00, 08:00 and so on. Olaf will take the first watch until midnight and then the middle watch will take over until 04:00 when the port watch will be on duty. If any enemy action is identified, raise the alarm and then it's all hands on deck."

Ragnar took over again.

"We know Whitelite have scuba equipment which means using scuba divers to attach the mine to our hull. I too keep scuba, DPV and ROV equipment in *Ravnsvart*'s boat house and Liv, Knut and Olaf are qualified as master divers. I have done a bit of diving too, so we can match them when it comes to diving."

Richard interrupted, "DPV? ROV? "

"*Å ja*, DPV; that means diver propulsion vehicle. It's a sort of battery powered underwater scooter, to increase range underwater and ROV means remotely operated underwater vehicle. It's a highly manoeuverable tethered underwater mobile device with a video camera and arms to carry out underwater tasks. Knut is an expert at handling the ROV. Actually we call it '*Rover*', our pet sea hound. These devices are standard equipment for our underwater engineering work.

"The Whitelite divers may come at us by road to Crinan, but they would be easily spotted. I think it more likely that they will be launched from *Whiteman Pioneer*. So the officer on watch should closely monitor her movements on AIS. And Knut, I want you to check over all the scuba equipment and make sure the DPV and *Rover* are fully charged and ready to go."

Hector nodded in admiration of Ragnar and his crew's thoroughness.

"So far so good, Ragnar, but what happens next – if and when Whitelite attack?"

This was the question everyone wanted to ask.

"*Godt spørsmål*, good question, Hector, good question." Ragnar paused. "The truth is, we will improvise. But we are expecting them and prepared. They don't know that. At all costs we look out for a scuba diver, or maybe more than one, let them attach the mine and then we detach it and if possible fix it to *Whiteman Pioneer*. As for what will happen, Fate will decide."

An apprehensive glum silence pervaded *Ravnsvart*'s dining area, until broken by Hector.

"I guess it's going to be a waiting game for a bit." He yawned. "I'm bushed. It's been a long day. I'm going to get some shut eye when I can."

Holly and Whisky followed suit and disappeared to their quarters. Whether sleep was uppermost in their thoughts may be left to the imagination.

Olaf, Richard and Frances made their way to the bridge to commence their watch and were quickly followed by Ragnar, who wanted to make sure everyone knew their role.

"The main thing for just now is to keep an eye on any movement by *Whiteman Pioneer* on the AIS; check the radar or by visual observation for any small craft movements that may be carrying a scuba diver or two and any suspicious lights or movements on shore. I doubt if divers would be willing to cover any great distance in the dark in these sea conditions."

Outside the warmth of the enclosed bridge, intermittent rain squalls lashed *Ravnsvart* and she tugged at her anchor cable as the wind whipped up the water of the sheltered Loch Crinan anchorage.

Ragnar made to depart through the bridge corridor, but turned and suggested, "Frances, why don't you get some rest? There's not much likely to happen for some time yet".

Frances gratefully took up the offer and went down to her snug state room and, despite the uncertainties facing all on board and the heaves and jerks as the ship rode to the gale, she fell into a deep sleep.

* * *

Olaf and Richard's watch was uneventful. Olaf had lent Richard a heavy weather waterproof jacket and they took alternate turns round the deck to check that all was well. It was, apart from the increasing gale, which in a way was a comfort. It would take a brave frogman indeed to swim through these wave tossed seas and strong currents in total darkness, to attach a limpet mine to *Ravnsvart*'s hull, without a give-away light.

Olaf and Richard were relieved at midnight by Ragnar, Whisky and Holly. Once again Ragnar suggested that Holly go below to rest until there might be more for her to do and indeed the midnight watch was equally uneventful.

At 04:00, the port watch relieved Ragnar and Whisky. In this case, all three of Liv, Knut and Hector opted to remain on duty. The routine of watching AIS and radar with periodic patrols round the deck continued without incident, until just after quarter past five.

Knut whispered, "Look, *Whiteman Pioneer* is moving".

HOSTILITIES COMMENCE

SURE enough, as all three looked at the screen, the little arrowhead representing *Whiteman Pioneer* had moved from her berthed position at Oban and had turned towards the sea. The read-out correctly showed the last port calls as Oban, Mallaig and Kyle of Lochalsh. No destination was indicated. As the enemy vessel moved out of the confines of Oban Bay, her course gradually backed and then hovered around 212°. Her speed was 7.8 knots.

Knut opened up the chart.

"See here, she's heading south towards us through Kerrera Sound. She'll keep her speed down until she's clear of Kerrera, then I think she'll open up. Her cruising speed is about 12 knots, 15 flat out. That means she should get here by sometime after 07:00. It looks like they are planning a dawn raid when they reckon we will be half asleep."

Hector examined the screen showing the sinister arrowhead moving inexorably southwards towards its impending encounter with *Ravnsvart*.

"I think we should let Ragnar know that the Illuminati are heading our way."

Liv countered, "No leave him until 06:30. There's nothing he can do for now. But Knut, get *Rover* and *Huginn* ready to launch at a moment's notice".

Knut jumped to this order and disappeared in the direction of the boat house.

Liv then added, "We'll keep an eye on the radar and continue our deck rounds just in case they attempt to approach us by a shore-based small craft."

There was no such activity, other than the fact that *Whiteman Pioneer* was now quite close, having just come through the Sound of Luing. At half past six Liv roused her father, explained the situation and went to her cabin to change into a wetsuit.

Ragnar joined Hector on the bridge, checked *Whiteman Pioneer*'s position and declared, "It's just about time for action stations, Hector. Go and wake everyone and get them to muster in the sky lounge".

Within quarter of an hour, Liv, now wetsuit attired, had returned to the bridge to resume watch. Everyone else had assembled in the sky lounge, on the same level, and amidships just aft of the bridge.

Ragnar commenced his briefing.

"Thank you all for being with me today. As you know we are in some peril but, if Fate is on our side, we shall pull through and vanquish an evil that is polluting our world. *Whiteman Pioneer* is less than half an hour's steaming from here. I think they will try to attack us as soon as there is enough light for a diver to see what he is doing. It's already starting to get light, so it's time for you to take your posts. Keep yourselves hidden and we'll douse all lights, except our riding lights to give the impression that the ship's company is asleep."

Ragnar then ordered each to various positions round the ship while Olaf Andersen and Frances had the task of providing tea, coffee and snacks, bacon rolls being generally popular. Otherwise to an outside observer that windy Saturday morning, *Ravnsvart* appeared lifeless as she lay at anchor.

As they waited, there was a lull in the gale. The sea was less agitated. Ragnar, Liv, and Hector were on the bridge awaiting events. The AIS display indicated that *Whiteman Pioneer* had rounded Craignish Point and was hove-to or anchored at the mouth of Loch Craignish, out

of sight and a couple of miles from *Ravnsvart*.
Meanwhile, on Ragnar's orders, Richard was at the boat
house helping Knut and Olaf fuel and launch the RIB
Huginn and tether her ready for action, should that be
necessary. *Rover*, the ROV, had also already been
prepared by Knut for immersion when the order was
given. Like Liv, Olaf had donned a wetsuit and turned his
hand to preparing two sets of scuba equipment. Having
done so, he returned to the bridge.

As daylight broke, the romantic outline of
Duntrune Castle dominated the northern shore of Loch
Crinan, a picturesque feature that would have captivated
the interest of those on *Ravnsvart*'s bridge had they not
been preoccupied with scanning the waters of the loch for
signs of enemy activity. Then a RIB appeared, at speed,
round Rubha na Moine, the northern headland that
separates Loch Crinan from the more open sea. Ragnar
followed the RIB through his powerful binoculars. It
carried two men. The little craft slowed, stopped, still
some way off from *Ravnsvart*, and one of the pair, in full
scuba gear dropped backwards into the sea, after which
the RIB accelerated away to disappear back round Rubha
na Moine.

Ragnar put down his binoculars.

"Right, the diver'll be here in ten minutes. Liv,
Olaf and Richard, make *Huginn* ready and we'll capture
the bastard. Richard, you take the helm and the radio. Liv,
Olaf be careful, but get him. Before you cast off, get Knut
to launch *Rover* and move it to *Ravnsvart*'s bow and
switch to bridge monitor. Hector, warn all hands to keep a
sharp look out for any sign of the diver and come running
here if they see anything."

With that each hurried to their posts. Liv, Olaf and Richard boarded *Huginn* and cast off ready to intercept. Knut appeared on the bridge with a 'box of tricks' and a monitor which he plugged into a socket. After keying in some codes, a visual image appeared on the monitor showing what *Rover*'s camera was picking up – green turbulent water and the outline of Ravnsvart's bow.

Ragnar peered at the screen.

"With these sea conditions, visibility is not good. Take *Rover* slowly down our starboard side. Knut manoeuvered the ROV thus – nothing but green water. Suddenly Holly burst into the bridge.

"I saw him out on our left side. He must have come up to see where he was – just his head and mask and then his flippers as he dived down again."

"Well done Holly."

"Knut, take Rover under *Ravnsvart* towards our port side and down to four metres with the camera looking upwards on wide angle."

Ragnar then took the radio mike.

"Bridge to *Huginn*, do you read me?"

"*Huginn* to bridge, Roger, I read you."

"Diver heading to ship's port side. Prepare to intercept – slowly – gently – until you have him."

"Aye aye sir."

Then Rover's camera, from its position almost under *Ravnsvart*, picked up the blurry outline of a diver swimming towards the ship's port side. When he reached *Ravnsvart*, he could be seen pulling something from a bag and attaching it to the hull about a metre below the waterline.

As this transpired, Ragnar took up the radio mike.

"Bridge to *Huginn*, he has placed the mine port side. Get him."

"Aye aye Sir."

Huginn had already moved stealthily towards the diver and, with a last spurt of the outboard, Olaf and Liv were in the water on top of the intruder. Liv grabbed his legs while Olaf pulled off the diver's mask and, with a serrated knife, cut his air pipe with an eruption of bubbles.

The diver desperately tried to fend off Olaf, but he was no match for the big Norwegian's brute strength. Liv managed to loop a line round the upper torso of the struggling figure, so that Richard was able to pull him to the surface spluttering and spouting sea water. Liv and Olaf surfaced beside him and secured his arms to prevent his escape.

Ragnar shouted from the bridge wing, "Get the bastard on board now."

As quickly as he could, Richard drove *Huginn* back to *Ravnsvart*'s stern platform, where Knut and Ragnar unceremoniously hauled the unfortunate diver out of the sea and pinned him down onto the stern platform.

Ragnar knelt and, with his face a foot from the diver, snarled, "How long before the mine goes off?"

The diver, white faced and terrified, snivelled, "about half an hour".

"Can it be deactivated? If it can't, you'll die here while the rest of us abandon ship."

"Yes, yes. It can be detached and I can deactivate it."

Liv, who was treading water and listening to this exchange shouted to Knut, "Get me a specimen net (of which there were several in the boat house) and I'll get the mine".

On receipt of the net Liv swam off, detached the limpet mine from *Ravnsvart*'s hull, delivered it to the stern platform and she and Olaf clambered aboard. A digital timer on the mine was counting down 00:17:23 – 22 – 21 – 20 .   .   .

Ragnar ordered everyone, except Knut, Hector, Liv and Olaf, to don life jackets and move right to the bow – just in case.

He then turned to the shivering diver.

"Now deactivate."

With trembling fingers, the diver keyed in a code and the digital timer stopped at 00:14:58.

INTERROGATION

THE limpet mine was rendered safe. With just fifteen minutes to spare, Ragner, Knut, Hector, Liv and Olaf breathed a collective sigh of relief, as no doubt did their prisoner, the hapless Whitelite diver.

Ragnar barked, "Get this *stygg stykke lur* up to the bridge deck lounge and we'll see what he has to say for himself. Leave the mine in the boat house for now where it can do least harm if anything goes wrong and Hector, get the rest of the ship's company to stand easy, but get them to keep a lookout as before".

Relieved of his scuba apparatus and with hands tied behind his back, the diver was frogmarched by Knut and Olaf up two deck levels to the sky lounge on the bridge deck. Ragnar followed behind with an underwater spear gun trained on the prisoner. On reaching the sky lounge, the diver's legs were also tied to prevent any attempt to escape. Ragnar then ordered Knut and Olaf to bring the RIB *Huginn* and the ROV *Rover* back on board and asked Liv to prepare *Ravnsvart* for sea as soon as she had changed out of her wetsuit.

With the spear gun aimed at the diver's groin, and in the presence of Hector, Ragnar eyed this sorry specimen who was trembling and almost in tears as he cowered against the bulkhead. He began the interrogation of his prisoner.

"Your name?"

He gave the diver a kick to encourage a quick response.

"H-H-Hunter, Harry Hunter."

"Now Harry, let's not waste time. We know all about Eva and Franklin's plan to blow up our beautiful ship. And, Harry, we caught you red-handed. So, Harry, we want information that we *don't* know. You'll help us with that, Harry, won't you?"

Ragnar gave the diver another kick.

"Y-Yes."

"First question: Are Eva Tillotson and Franklin Hendrix on board *Whitelite Pioneer* now?"

"Yes."

"Besides blowing us up, what do they plan to do?"

"They are going to wreck your experimental tidal stream arrays."

"Are they, now? How interesting Harry. Not a very nice thing to do, is it?"

"No," Harry whimpered.

Ragnar gave Harry another kick.

"I didn't hear you."

"No. It's not."

"Who killed Councillor Ewan MacLeod?

"It was Reg Pemberton. He does all Franklin's dirty work."

"Yes. We knew that. Just testing that you are telling the truth. And Lachie Mackinnon?"

"It was Reg Pemberton too. He killed Mackinnon."

"Quite so. Quite so. Who killed my wife?"

"I don't know. I wasn't around at the time, but I heard that Eva Tillotson organized it and the 'accident' was meant for you, not your wife. Eva was in trouble for not getting you."

"The death of my wife upset me greatly. Can you imagine that Harry?"

Harry made no answer.

Ragnar gave the now sobbing diver another kick.

"Can you imagine Harry? Can you?"

"N-No. I'm sorry."

"*You're* sorry. *You're* sorry. You miserable fucker. Not half as sorry as you will be when I've finished with you."

At this point Ragnar, his Odinist blood now boiling, was about to throttle the whimpering diver, but Hector intervened.

"Easy Ragnar. Easy. I'd like to ask Harry something of more immediate concern."

Hector then addressed Harry Hunter in more moderate terms.

"We watched your RIB drop you off just this side of the headland and then head back from where it had come. Once you had fixed the limpet mine on *Ravnsvart*'s hull, how did you plan to get back to *Whiteman Pioneer*? It's a long swim and there are very nasty currents outside the loch here."

"I was to swim to the shore by the headland. There's a little inlet on the other side where our RIB is waiting to pick me up."

"So, they'll be wondering why you haven't turned up and why there has been no big bang? It should have gone off by now, shouldn't it?"

"Yes."

"What do you think they'll do now?"

"I don't know. They'll probably hang around for a while and then maybe they'll come to investigate."

Ragnar, having regained his cool, joined in.

"All right Harry Hunter. That's enough for just now. We're keeping you here until we hand you over to the police. I don't think we should hang around too much longer in case your gang start to think up more mischief.

He then turned to Hector.

"Why don't you make yourself comfortable and take a seat with the spear gun pointed at our friend here. If

185

he moves, let him have it where it hurts. I'll go and see how our preparations for sea are getting on."

Another thought occurred to Ragnar. He turned and asked one more question of Harry Hunter:

"What are the codes to activate and de-activate the mine? You'd better tell the truth or you'll be blown sky high with the rest of us."

Harry paused open mouthed and Ragnar made to grab his neck.

"All right I'll tell you. I'll tell you. It's 6666 to activate and 9999 to de-activate."

SEA CHASE

W HILE the ship's company was busy making ready for sea, stowing *Huginn* and *Rover*, the scuba equipment and other paraphernalia, the lull in the gale had passed and the wind had picked up again with a new fury.

At last all was ready and in order. With Liv at the helm the anchor was weighed and, even before the *Ravnsvart* had turned seaward, the Whitelite RIB appeared round Rubha na Moine, its sole occupant presumably seeking the missing diver and trying to ascertain why the motor yacht was still in one piece. As it was immediately clear to him that *Ravnsvart* was under way, the RIB circled and sped off in the direction of the mother ship amid a flurry of spray as it was buffeted by the breaking waves.

Ragnar smiled a grim smile, but said nothing.

A north westerly course was set towards the Dorus Mòr. *Ravnsvart*'s bow punched into the troughs between the breaking swells and sent feathers of spray over the bridge windows. Within a few minutes, as *Ravnsvart* approached the islet called Eilean nan Coinean, that marks the mouth of Loch Sween, *Whiteman Pioneer* hove into sight. She too was under way and heading south west at speed on a collision course with *Ravnsvart*.

"She's trying to ram us," shouted Ragnar. "Make full speed."

Liv pushed the twin throttles all the way forward and *Ravnsvart* surged ahead, pitching violently into the waves as her powerful engines thrust her forward with the engines racing flat-out. Green water gushed over the foredeck with each dive, to be shed as the bow rose to the next swell. Elsewhere on board, the sound of crashing crockery mingled with the cries of those thrown off their feet by the violent motion.

Ravnsvart's sudden spurt of speed took *Whiteman Pioneer*'s helmsman by surprise. He turned to starboard, to try to inflict a glancing blow, but missed, passing within a couple of feet of *Ravnsvart*'s stern.

"Wow, that was close," gasped Richard, who had come up to the bridge to see what was happening.

Ragnar looked back at *Whiteman Pioneer* which had continued her starboard turn and was now following closely in *Ravnsvart*'s wake.

"We'll soon pull away from her. We have much more power and speed, but it'll be pretty uncomfortable. Richard, can you check up on everyone to see if they are all right?"

The ship pitched violently, while Richard headed carefully back down the bridge corridor.

As Ragnar had predicted, *Ravnsvart* pulled steadily away from *Whiteman Pioneer* as the powerful twin diesels pushed her forward into the crashing seas. As they approached Dorus Mòr, however, the narrow passage between the Mainland's Craignish Point and the island of Garbh Rèisa, all on board experienced a lurch forward as *Ravnsvart* suddenly decelerated and turned sharply to port.

The port engine rev indicator sank to zero. That engine had cut out.

Liv turned the helm a-starboard to compensate, thereby narrowly avoiding running aground on the island.

Ragnar made his way as fast as he could to the Engine room, where Knut was already trying to fathom out what was wrong with the now inactive port engine.

"What the Hell's happened?"

Knut was, as normal, wearing ear defenders against the din of the still roaring starboard engine and although he could not hear Ragnar's actual words, he knew well enough his concern.

He shouted, "blocked oil filter I think".

"How long to fix?"

Knut shrugged and answered in Norwegian, "*en halv time – kanskje*" (half an hour – maybe).

"Do you need help?"

"No. Quicker on my own."

With that Ragnar made his way back to the bridge, observing as he went that *Whiteman Pioneer* was following about four cable lengths behind.

Back on the bridge he asked Liv for a progress report.

"We are down to about thirteen or fourteen knots. The starboard helm and dead prop are acting as brakes and the wind is now storm force. I'd say *Whiteman Pioneer* is gaining on us slightly."

Richard had also returned to the bridge reporting that everyone was more or less all right apart from a few bruises and some cases of seasickness. The sudden lurch caused by the port engine failure had almost made Hector involuntarily shoot Harry Hunter, but fortunately he managed not to.

Ragnar paused and considered for one long minute. Then he decided.

"We make for Corryvreckan."

He then turned to Richard.

"Come with me. We're going to stop that bastard."

The pair hurried aft and down to the boat house, where Olaf was still sorting through and stowing some of the equipment that had been disturbed during the earlier hurried quest for scuba and other gear.

"Let's have a look at that mine."

Ragnar inspected the limpet mine and pondered the quarter of an hour reading on the timer. He then rummaged round some of the equipment that Olaf had been so carefully stowing. He picked up a spherical float, of the type lobstermen use, and as also used by Ragnar's team to mark underwater tidal stream measuring apparatus.

"Ah. This should work. If we attach the mine to this float and then tie the float to a long line, we can send our friends in *Whiteman Pioneer* a nice early Christmas present."

Richard mulled over the moral dilemma that this proposed course of action presented. On the one hand, to float the mine back to the following ship would almost certainly result in the deaths of those on board. On the other hand, it was clear that the Whitelite people were still intent on destroying *Ravnsvart* and those on board, so he concluded that Ragnar's proposal was a justifiable case of self-defence.

"We will need to reset the timer," Richard added, "And to do that we will need the co-operation of our prisoner."

Ragnar chuckled. "Ah ha, I already have that. Its 6666 to activate and 9999 to deactivate – simple enough – so long as we don't hold the thing upside down. We have a quarter of an hour between re-setting the timer and floating the mine back to *Whiteman Pioneer*."

Olaf meanwhile secured the mine to the float with twine and duct tape and then located a long line coiled at the back of the boat house. He bent one end of the line to

the float and Ragnar keyed in the activate code 6666 and the count-down recommenced – 00:14:57 – 56 – 55 – 54 .
. .

While Ragnar, Olaf and Richard were preparing these countermeasures, *Ravnsvart* and *Whiteman Pioneer* had reached the entrance to the infamous Gulf of Corryvreckan. Had the majority of those on board been aware of the warnings in the Admiralty Sailing Directions, they would have been even more anxious than they already were. As Liv already knew, these directions pointed out that '*passage through the gulf from E to W is more dangerous than a passage in the opposite direction*' and they stressed '*nor should passage be attempted with wind against the tide.*'

Not only was *Ravnsvart* heading in the more dangerous east to west direction, but was proceeding into a westerly storm set against a maximum strength west going spring tide with one engine out of action – the very worst of circumstances.

On the bridge Liv piloted her ship into what seemed like a boiling cauldron of white foaming swirling water. The ship pitched and bucked, twisted and slewed violently and it was with the utmost difficulty that Liv was able to fight the ship's tendency to spin out of control, a problem exacerbated by the outing of the port engine. She kept as close as she reasonably could to the Jura shore and all the time *Whiteman Pioneer* followed, gradually gaining on *Ravnsvart*.

Back at the boat house, Ragnar had opened the stern door and tied the free end of the long line to a cleat on the stern platform. The violent motion of the ship made it difficult for the three men to keep their balance. Swirling water washed the pitching stern platform dangerously, but Ragnar began streaming the line with its deadly payload in *Ravnsvart*'s wake until he judged that the mine was close to *Whitelight Pioneer*. He then looped the line round the cleat to make it fast.

He stood up and checked his balance, when a bullet ricocheted off the top coaming of the boat-house. A second bullet caught Ragnar on the thigh. He fell and a wave washed him right to the edge of the platform, his legs dangling over the brink. He was on the verge of falling to his death into the boiling wake, but Richard just managed to grab his arm. He too was in danger of being pulled backwards over the edge, were it not that his other hand was in turn held firm by Olaf who was able to gain purchase on the cleat. With immense strength, Olaf held the combined weight of Richard and Ragnar.

Another bullet whistled past them.

Ravnsvart bucked in the swirl of a great eddy. The three men held on and in the succeeding roll Ragnar was hauled back from the brink.

Olaf and Richard were then able to drag Ragnar into the safety of the boathouse.

There, lying prone on the deck, gasping for breath, the three men stared back at the encroaching enemy when a huge column of spray erupted just aft of *Whiteman Pioneer*'s stern. The mine had exploded.

But still the enemy ship pressed on towards them, apparently undamaged.

Half a minute later the line to which the mine had been attached suddenly tautened and snapped, the free end whipping dangerously above their heads. Then a strange thing happened. *Whiteman Pioneer* veered to starboard and gradually receded from *Ravnsvart*'s wake.

"My God the line must have fouled her propellers."

As they watched the hated ship, she was being drawn broadside towards the Hag, that most deadly of Corryvreckan's whirlpools. The Hag drew her closer and closer. She listed more and more and then her stern was awash. She twisted and spun until the Hag pulled the stricken vessel and all of her crew to the depths.

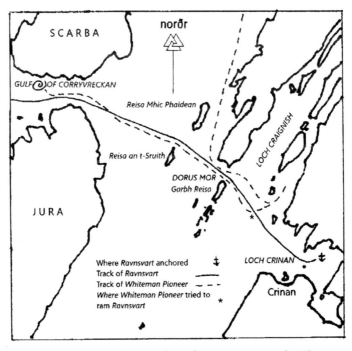

Chart showing the tracks of Ravnsvart and Whiteman Pioneer

THE odd thing is that, apart from the three men in the boat-house, almost no one else on board *Ravnsvart* saw the demise of *Whiteman Pioneer*. Liv, on the bridge, with eyes forward, was concentrating on steering a course through the angry, foaming and unpredictable waters of the Gulf of Corryvreckan. Knut was in the engine room, splattered with oil, in the process of changing the port engine's oil filter. Holly was dreadfully seasick and had taken to her cabin. Frances too was in her stateroom, not seasick as such, but queasy and lying on her bed as more comfortable than fighting the ship's violent motion on foot. Also feeling nauseous, Hector, in the sky lounge, spear gun in hand, was diligently keeping an eye on Harry Hunter.

Only Whisky, John Walker, son of a now retired Royal Naval Commander, had gone up to the flying bridge to glory in the elemental fury of Corryvreckan. The spray broke over him and stung his face, but despite the danger presented by both the evil intent of those on *Whiteman Pioneer* and the perils of Corryvreckan itself, he had never felt more alive. He had looked alternately forward at the boiling water of the gulf and back at the progress of the enemy vessel when he saw the tower of spray followed by the muffled 'thrump' of the exploding mine. Then he watched spellbound as the white ship lost steerage way and fell victim to the insatiable Hag.

Whisky left the flying bridge and made his way through the sky lounge, past Hector and Harry Hunter, to the bridge to check whether or not Liv had seen the foundering of *Whitelite Pioneer*. On the answer being negative, he reported the spectacle he had observed.

Captain Liv Torkelsen was quick to respond.

"Go check on my father and Richard. They should be in the boathouse."

This Whisky did, informing Hector (and Harry) of the news in the passing. On reaching the boat house he found the three men still gasping and recovering from their efforts. Whisky was horrified to learn that Ragnar had been shot.

Richard was the first to speak.

"Look, we must get Ragnar to his stateroom and get Frances to look at him. She's a trained nursing sister."

The mighty Olaf said nothing, but gently lifted Ragnar bodily onto his shoulder and carried him up the swaying companionway, through the lounge and along the corridor to the luxurious master stateroom where he placed his wounded boss carefully on the double bed.

Richard, meanwhile, roused Frances and escorted her to Ragnar's bedside.

Frances took charge of matters from that point. After a quick assessment, she asked Olaf to bring the ship's first aid kit. While he was fetching this, she removed Ragnar's jacket and trousers, washed her hands in the adjacent bathroom, and inspected the wound.

"Nasty flesh wound. At least the femoral artery has not been severed. If it had you would have bled to death in two minutes."

Ragnar, who was in some pain, managed a half smile.

"It's a while since I let a woman take off my trousers." He added, "Or anyone else for that matter."

Olaf returned with the first aid kit. Frances inspected its contents, cleaned the wound with disinfectant as best she could and applied a dressing and bandage. She then made Ragnar comfortable, pulled the bed covers up and made him take two pain killers, washed down by water from a glass that Richard had fetched from the bathroom.

In a comforting, but strict nursing voice, Sister Frances soothed, "Now, be a good boy and get some sleep."

Frances then turned to Olaf and suggested that he inform Liv that her father had been wounded, but that she believed he would be all right, so long as he received proper medical attention. Big man that he was, Olaf was streaming with tears, partly of distress at the suffering of his boss and partly relief that it seemed he was going to recover from his trauma. Olaf complied immediately and made his way to the bridge.

While Frances mopped Ragnar's brow, Richard noticed that the ship's violent pitching and slewing motion had changed to a more regular heave and roll.

"If you're all right for just now, I'm going up to the bridge to see what's happening."

When Richard reached the bridge, Olaf had taken over the helm and Liv was giving him orders as to course and speed. She turned to Richard.

"We're through Corryvrecken. Things should be a bit easier now. I'm going down to see my father. Olaf says that he going to be okay – thank God."

Liv left to attend to her father.

Now that *Ravnsvart* was on the open sea and clear of the treacherous Corryvreckan whirlpools, Olaf reduced speed to ease the strain on the racing starboard engine and to lessen the violence of the ship's motion. Liv had ordered Olaf to take *Ravnsvart* northwest, well clear of a lee shore, before heading north eastward up the Firth of Lorne to Oban where it was hoped proper medical attention could be secured for Ragnar.

It was not long after Richard had joined Olaf on the bridge that an oil spattered Knut appeared, to announce that he had changed the blocked oil filter and that the port engine was ready to be started. Olaf pressed the self-start button and the rev indicator displayed tick-over. Olaf then pushed the port throttle forward and pulled the starboard throttle back so that both engines were running at the same moderate speed. With normal propulsion restored, steering immediately became easier.

Ravnsvart was still punching into heavy seas, but the wind was backing to a more southwesterly direction, which caused the ship to roll as well as pitch. Thinking of Ragnar's comfort, Olaf turned *Ravnsvart*'s bow northeast, Oban bound and, at once, with a now following wind, the motion eased. The swells were as large as before, but the ship was now running with them, instead of against them. The big motor yacht was virtually surfing towards the fairway of the Firth of Lorne. Olaf pushed the throttles forward to increase speed.

"We should be in Oban in just over an hour."

Twenty minutes later, Liv returned to the bridge, she was clearly anxious about her father.

"The sooner we get him to a doctor the better."

She then took up the radio mike and contacted Oban harbour on channel 16. On making contact she informed the harbour master's office that the owner of the vessel had a serious gunshot wound that needed urgent medical attention and that they had apprehended an individual who had attempted murder. She also asked the harbour office to pass on the intelligence that the motor ship *Whiteman Pioneer* had foundered in the Gulf of Corryverckan, with the presumed loss of all hands.

With both Liv and Olaf on the bridge, Richard decided to see how Frances was managing with Ragnar's care. Before doing so, he went to the sky lounge to check on Hector and the prisoner, there to discover that Whisky had taken Hector's place.

"Hector was feeling sick, so I sent him to his stateroom to lie down. Things seem to have settled down a bit now. How are we doing?"

"We should be in Oban soon, so we can hand over Harry here to the police."

Then, addressing Harry directly, Richard in simple monkish goodness advised, "Look Harry, if you tell the truth to the police, it will be easier for you in the long run. Whitelite are finished, *Whiteman Pioneer* is at the bottom of the sea. There were no survivors. You are lucky to be alive. Make a clean breast of it."

Harry whimpered, "They've no more hold over me now. They made me fix the mine. I didn't want to do it."

Richard then went down to the spacious owner's stateroom where Frances was sitting beside a sleeping Ragnar.

"He's resting, but he needs to get that wound attended to by a doctor. How long before we're in port?"

"Oh, about half an hour, I suppose."

Richard sat for a while with Frances and then returned to the sky lounge. He took the spear gun from Whisky.

"I think we'll put this back in the boat house. Harry's going to do the right thing now."

Richard took the weapon to the boathouse and returned to the bridge.

Soon thereafter *Ravnsvart* rounded the north end of Kerrera, entered Oban Bay and, as instructed by the harbour master's office, headed for the wet and windswept North Pier, whereon was assembled an ambulance, a police van, two police cars, Inspector MacGillivray and five other police officers, two of whom were armed.

TROUBLE WITH THE LAW

O N that late and eventful Saturday morning, the sight of an ambulance on the quay was a comfort to Liv and others aboard *Ravnsvart*. The size and nature of the police presence, however, seemed excessive for the arrest of one individual who had already been subdued.

Lines were presented fore and aft by Olaf and Knut respectively, made fast by shore personnel and *Ravnsvart* was securely berthed at Oban's North Pier. A gangway was dragged between pier and the ship's quarter deck, made fast and Inspector MacGillivray stood at the shore end of it flanked by the two armed officers.

Liv had come down from the bridge and walked the length of the gangway.

"Good morning officer, I presume you have come to arrest our prisoner Harry Hunter."

The inspector frowned, "Harry Hunter? No, we know nothing of a Harry Hunter. I have a warrant to arrest Ragnar Torkelsen. I must instruct the captain of this ship to hand him over immediately."

"*I* am Captain Liv Torkelsen. Ragnar Torkelsen is my father. He is severely injured with a gunshot wound and needs immediate medical attention.

"The man you need to arrest is Harry Hunter. He attempted to blow up this vessel with all on board early this morning, and would have been successful had we not stopped him and deactivated the limpet mine that he had fixed to our hull. That was attempted murder plus piracy, terrorism and whatever else you want to add. We radioed to the harbour office here that we had apprehended this person."

Inspector MacGillivray was taken aback, firstly that the captain of this luxury yacht was a young, assertive and attractive blond-haired woman and, secondly that she was insisting that he arrest someone completely different from the person named on the warrant he carried.

"But we got a message from the harbour office that you had indicated that someone had been shot and the owner was involved. We understand that Ragnar Torkelsen is the owner and we have been informed that he murdered Councillor Ewan MacLeod and Lachlan Mackinnon."

By this time Olaf, Richard, Hector and Holly were on the quarterdeck and flabbergasted at the accusation. Hector nearly exploded:

"This is utter baloney. Ragnar had nothing to do with these deaths. Those murders were committed by Reg Pemberton."

Richard joined the fray in more measured tones.

"Inspector MacGillivray, Ragnar *saved* me and my good lady from being killed by that thug Pemberton."

The inspector took off his hat and pushed back his hair in frustration.

"Who is this Reg Pemberton?

Hector snapped, "An employee of Whitelite Power. If you want to do your job properly, *he's* the one you need to arrest, along with Harry Hunter, who we have on board – also an employee of Whitelite Power". He paused, and then added, "And, unless you want to add another death to the total, Ragnar needs to get to a doctor or hospital pretty damn quick!"

Inspector MacGillivray was in a quandary. Leaving the armed officers at the head of the gangway, he went to the ambulance, spoke to the paramedics, who had remained in their vehicle sheltering from the wind and rain, brought them to the gangway and addressed Liv.

"Where is Ragnar Torkelsen – your father?"

"He is in his state room, sedated."

"Show us the way."

Liv stood her ground, flanked by the burly Olaf and the oil spattered Knut with large spanner in hand, and insisted, "This is a Norwegian vessel. I am the master and *I* determine who boards my ship. However, we wish to co-operate with the police and you and the two ambulance men may come aboard."

Liv ushered the three gentlemen up the gangway and showed them the way down to the main deck and Ragnar's luxurious state room.

There he lay on his bed, asleep, with Frances sitting by his side.

Frances rose, greeted the paramedics, while ignoring the police inspector.

"Ah, good. You've arrived. I did my best to clean and dress the wound, but it needs professional attention. I'm worried about sepsis."

The ambulance men drew down the bed covers and inspected Frances's dressing.

"That's grand for now miss. You've done a neat job. We'll move him onto the stretcher and get him to hospital."

The paramedics slid the now wakening, but dozy, Ragnar onto the stretcher, carried him back through the ship's saloon and dining area to the after companionway, up onto the quarterdeck and across the gangway to the waiting ambulance. Inspector MacGillivray followed them, detaching one of the unarmed officers as he went to accompany and guard 'the casualty'. The ambulance then sped off to the Lorn and Islands District General Hospital, located on the southern outskirts of Oban.

Liv had sought to accompany her father to the hospital but had been prevented by the inspector.

"As you can see, I have placed an armed guard at the gangplank. No one may leave this boat without my authority."

Richard winced at the landlubberly reference to *Ravnsvart* as a 'boat', but said nothing.

Liv, who was becoming angry at the police treatment of *Ravnsvart*'s complement, and of her father in particular, protested.

"What the Hell is going on here. You accuse my father of murder, when he has been doing all he can to *prevent* the deaths of innocent people. We hold an attempted murderer on board and you show no interest in taking him off our hands. Is this the best the Scottish Police can do? I am not impressed."

Inspector MacGillivray flushed, but held firm.

"Captain Torkelsen, if you will make space available on board for my sergeant and me to interview each member of your crew in turn, then perhaps we can get to the facts."

This was agreed.

Liv, Olaf, Hector and Richard escorted the inspector and his sergeant (Sergeant Nicolson, whom Richard and Frances has previously met at Shona's guest house) to the sky lounge. There, of course, seated, were Whisky and Harry Hunter, whose legs had been unbound by Whisky in anticipation of his departure into police custody, but whose hands were still tied.

203

Liv made a deliberate show of formally introducing the pair.

"May I introduce John Walker, otherwise known as Whisky, and our – what can I say – detainee, Harry Hunter."

Whisky stood up.

"Oh, at last. You've come to take Harry away. He wants to go to the toilet, but I couldn't let him – in case . . . Well, now we have police guards, it's okay."

Still in his diving suit, Harry stood up. Without waiting for approval, Whisky untied Harry's hands and showed him to the adjacent toilet.

In Harry's temporary absence, Liv advised, "You can hold your interviews here if you like. We can move Harry somewhere else for now but the sooner we get him off the ship, the better". She thought for a few seconds and then added, "I suggest you start with me. I have been with my father since we entered Scottish waters".

Events were moving faster that the inspector wished, but, for want of a better strategy, he had little option but to agree.

"Very well Captain, we will start with you."

At this point Harry reappeared from the toilet convoyed by Whisky.

Liv again took charge.

"We can put Harry in the bridge for now. Whisky needs a break. We'll put Harry under the watch of Hector and Olaf, but inspector, don't you think he should be handcuffed?"

It was of course not Liv's place to make such suggestions and the inspector dismissed it with a sharp, "That won't be necessary unless and until I caution and arrest this man".

In a sarcastic aside Hector opined, "I would have though attempted murder would be reason enough, but of course inspector, you know best".

Olaf and Hector escorted Harry to the bridge and admittedly, it would have taken a brave man to have taken on a bear like Olaf.

Inspector MacGillivray glowered at Hector and sighed impatiently. He pointed to one of the seats at a round table, whereat Liv sat down. The inspector and sergeant took seats opposite. The latter produced a digital recording device and placed it on the table. With a nod from Liv, Richard who had remained thus far in the sky lounge, absented himself to join the others in the saloon.

"Right, Captain Torkelsen, maybe now we can make a start."

POLICE DELIBERATIONS AND SHIPBOARD ACTIVITIES

I T would be tedious to provide a verbatim report of the ensuing interviews with Captain Liv Torkelsen and others. The activities of the main characters and sequence of events leading up to *Ravnsvart*'s arrival in Oban have already been described. In summary, however, it is worth noting the following particulars.

The questioning of Liv took longer than Inspector MacGillivray and Sergeant Nicolson had originally assumed. At several points Liv had to go back in time to explain events that had happened in Norway that were relevant to explain more recent circumstances. After an hour or so, the questioning broke off for lunch – a wholesome soup and sandwich affair that had been prepared by Frances and Holly, now hungry, having more or less recovered from her seasickness. All on board were provided with this fare including Harry Hunter. Even the armed police on shore were offered this bounty.

During this short break, Liv retrieved the sound file that Jimmy Ritchie had emailed of the conversation between Hendrix and Eva Tillotson in which the bumping off of 'that councillor' and the intention to 'blow him and his yacht up' eres alluded to. She transferred it to her laptop. After the interview recommenced, at the appropriate moment Liv played the recording to the astonishment of the two policemen.

The interview concluded mid-afternoon with Liv's description of the frustrated attempt by Harry Hunter to plant the limpet mine and the ensuing sea chase, in the course of which *Whiteman Pioneer* had attempted to ram and subsequently fired on *Ravnsvart*, which led to the wounding of her father. She could not provide details of *Whiteman Pioneer*'s foundering, as she had not personally witnessed it.

At Liv's suggestion, the next to be interviewed was Hector. He described the events in Vancouver that had led his company had almost been ruined by the Whiteman Corporation and which resulted in his coming to Scotland in support of Ragnar. Hector also described the confession that had been extracted from Harry Hunter through which Reg Pemberton had been confirmed as the murderer of Councillor MacLeod and Lachie Mackinnon.

When the inspector and sergeant had finished interviewing Hector, they decided to postpone further interviews until the following day. They were sufficiently persuaded as to Harry Hunter's misdeeds that he was cautioned and arrested on suspicion of attempted murder.

The armed guard was stood down, but on police orders, *Ravnsvart*'s complement was still not permitted to go ashore. Not even Liv was allowed to visit her father in hospital. The interviews were to resume the following morning.

A sense of frustration pervaded the ship. Not only were those on board worried about Ragnar in terms of both the prognosis for his recovery and especially about the unjust charge of murder. The despondency was relieved to some extent, however, as the evening wore on, by a healthy Norwegian style stew, followed by a session of stories and music. The adventures of the previous twenty-four hours were recalled, almost with disbelief, not least at the negative attitude of the police. In due course a keyboard was extracted from somewhere among the ships stores, by the normally quiet, but now spruced up Knut. He proceeded to accompany himself on a selection of popular songs with a surprisingly mellow singing voice – for a ships engineer, as Liv remarked. Frances then took over with Irish songs in both Gaelic and English. Holly told the tale of the Elven Knight[13], Richard sang a couple of Devon sea shanties, Hector described the origins of the Green Douglas Clan of which he was the chiefain, and Whisky sang Donnelly Dolan's recent hit Moonshine Girl. Then, unaccompanied, Olaf sang a Norwegian drinking song in a rich baritone voice that sank to such a low note that Frances speculated as to whether he was in danger of pooping his pants. This raised a laugh, not least by Olaf himself.

* * *

By the following morning the storm had blown itself out. The sky had brightened and Oban and its bay had taken on more of the picturesque character for which it was famous. Ferries which had been cancelled on the previous day were once again sailing to schedule. Stormbound fishing boats had already headed to sea or were about to.

After a late Sunday breakfast it was all hands to sprucing up the ship. Tasks included washing the salt off the superstructure and plate glass windows, swabbing the decks, polishing the bright-work, vacuuming, dusting and polishing in the saloons, a process that kept everyone busy until lunch time.

---

[13] The tale of the Elven Knight is narrated in Sweetheart Murder, ISBN: 978-905787-93-7

It was not until about two o'clock in the afternoon that Inspector MacGillivray and Sergeant Nicolson arrived. The inspector announced, "Captain Torkelsen, you will be pleased to learn that the charge against your father has been dropped. You are now free to visit him if you wish. In fact, once we have completed our questions, you are all free to leave the boat."

At this news, Liv immediately put Olaf in charge of *Ravnsvart*, went to her cabin to don a top coat and left the ship in search of a taxi to take her to the hospital.

The inspector then addressed those remaining.

"My sergeant and I will now question each of you in turn."

They commenced this procedure with Olaf and Knut, who's normally fluent English had unaccountably left them, so that they affected difficulty in understanding the policemen's questions or questionrd each other in Norwegian to find suitable vocabulary to answer. Coming to the conclusion that the two 'simple' sailors had no information of value to add to the case notes, they were quickly dismissed.

Next for questioning were Holly and Whisky. Once again, as very recent guests on board Ravnsvart, they had little fresh information to divulge other than corroboration of facts already gleaned. Once again the interview was brief.

Lastly came Richard and Frances who, of course, the two policemen had already met at Shona MacLeod's guest house. Their questioning took rather longer, as it involved descriptions of their movements since that last meeting.

Once he was satisfied that he had a full understanding of the facts, the inspector adopted a rather stern demeanor.

"You will both recall that when we met previously, I instructed you not to leave Skye and I understand that in aiding your departure from the island, Mrs – em – McGarrigle, that your landlady impersonated a police woman. This is a serious offence which I will have to consider. There may, however, be mitigating circumstances in this case, but in future I strongly advise you both to follow police procedures."

To this last comment, Richard countered, "If we had followed police procedures, we would now be dead."

The inspector made no reply, but had to admit inwardly that the ex-monk was right.

Having completed their questioning, the police left the ship and Olaf announced, "Why don't you all go ashore for a couple of hours? I'll stay on board to guard the ship."

After being cooped up on board for so long, the suggestion was very much welcomed. The last couple of days had taken it out of Frances, however. She was tired and opted to rest. The others trouped ashore.

It being Sunday and off season, many of the shops were closed, but a stroll along the waterfront to stretch their legs was much appreciated. Richard walked as far as the Roman Catholic Cathedral of Argyll and the Isles, which he entered for a brief commune with his God.

Liv returned to *Ravnsvart* at about six o'clock to announce that she had spent some time with her father, that he had responded well to treatment and was asking after all of them. To celebrate Ragnar's favourable prognosis and their relief from police suspicions, Liv declared that she wished to take everyone out that evening to a hotel for a meal. Frances was not hungry and still fatigued and Richard opted to stay with her while the others went out.

Later, Frances had a notion for sardines on toast. The ship was well stocked with tinned sardines, they being a common Norwegian product, and Richard joined her in this simple repast.

The rest of the ship's company returned quite late, in high spirits and somewhat inebriated. Thus concluded the events of that Sunday in Oban.

HOMEWARD BOUND

THE next morning, it being Monday, "home" was in the minds of each individual on board that comfortable motor yacht with which, in the course of their collective travails, they had formed a firm bond. Phone calls were made to re-establish contact with the outside world and preparations were made to pack by those who were leaving *Ravnsvart* later that day.

One important duty remained and that was the collective desire by Hector, Whisky, Holly, Richard and Frances to visit Ragnar, check on his progress and say their farewells. A minibus was ordered and by half past ten this group had descended on the Lorn and Islands Hospital. It was fortunate that visiting rules were relatively relaxed and all were admitted to Ragnar's bedside.

It was noted with some pleasure that the patient seemed bright eyed and alert. The staff nurse confirmed that the big Norwegian was on the mend, but that it would take time before he was fighting fit. When she learned that Frances had carried out the initial cleaning and dressing of the wound, she commended her thoroughness. It transpired that the staff nurse was from Barra in the Outer Hebrides and, on learning that Frances was, herself, a former nursing sister and from Donegal, they had a friendly, if brief, exchange in Gaelic. As part of this conversation, the staff nurse confirmed that Mr Torkelsen would be kept in the hospital for another night, but, all being well, allowed out the following morning.

Ragnar explained to the others that, because of his condition, the hospital staff had not permitted the police to question him until just before lunch-time on the previous day and that, in the course of the interview, to confirm his innocence and to demonstrate the guilt of Reg Pemberton, he had pointed them towards the evidence that Jimmie Ritchie held. Particularly damning were two images that Professor Einar Lund had taken of email print outs that had been lying carelessly in the back of the Whitelite Range Rover, presumably as an instruction from Eva to the pair in the Range Rover. These were firstly an acknowledgement that Reg Pemberton had 'bumped off' Councillor MacLeod and secondly an instruction to Eva to kill 'the fisherman' and 'the monk' and his wife as well, just to make sure. Leaving these documents in view was an extraordinarily careless slip-up by Franklin Hendrix.

Ragnar was, however, keen to know more detail of what had transpired with regard to the police on the previous two days. This was summarized by each giving his or her account of events.

It was Richard who volunteered, "What I still can't understand is why the police were so convinced that you had murdered Ewan MacLeod and Lachie Mackinnon".

Ragnar smiled.

"Ah ha, I've worked that one out. Eva – the evil bitch – Tillotson was behind it. I'm absolutely sure of it. The phone call Hector made to her, pretending to be one of the Illuminati, must have scared the shits out of her. She must have contacted the police immediately after, with damned lies to – what's the phrase? – to frame me. She probably assumed that we would all be dead by now. In the end Fate has saved us and doomed Evil Eva and her crew. My death moot is over.

The little group then explained that they would be leaving *Ravnsvart* that day to head for home and wanted to thank Ragnar and his crew for their hospitality and wish him a speedy recovery and safe passage back to Norway.

Ragnar in turn was quite moved and disappointed by the fact that his new friends would be departing so soon.

"I can only say this. It is I who must give you my heartfelt thanks for coming to my aid. Without you we would never have overcome the Illuminati-inspired menace. Thank you all very much."

With that they left the hospital and returned to *Ravnsvart*.

Hector, Holly and Whisky had just time to catch the stylish red, yellow and white 12:10 West Coast Motors Glasgow bus. Frances and Richard went to see them off although they would all meet again soon at Dalmannoch.

Frances and Richard had not long returned to *Ravnsvart*, when a yellow Renault Megane drew up on the quayside. It was Frances's car from which emerged the Reverend Donald Angus MacLeod.

Frances clapped her hands.

"Oh Donald, how wonderful to see you. And the car. Why don't you come aboard for a bite of lunch?"

Thus their means of travelling back to Dalmannoch was manifest. Donald had, as requested earlier by phone, gathered up and stowed Richard's clothes, pyjamas, and bathroom requisites together with a few things that Frances had left behind at Shona's guest house. Over lunch, to his astonishment, Richard and

Frances updated Donald on everything that had happened since he had left them at Iona.

"Wow, some adventure, I'm rather jealous that I couldn't take part."

"Well", admitted Richard, "I have to admit there were some pretty scary moments. I don't know that I'd like to repeat the experience in a hurry."

At this point Liv joined them and was informed that the Rev had delivered Frances' car to enable their journey home.

"Good to see you again, Reverend MacLeod. Welcome back on board." She continued, "I have just been to the harbour office to settle our harbour dues. I now know why our radio message on Saturday got mixed up. It seems that the normally efficient harbour master was on leave for a few days and was temporarily replaced by a young clerk from the council who was – how can I put it – out of his depth. That certainly didn't help matters did it?"

Liv pondered for a minute and then turned again to the Rev.

"Tell me, Reverend MacLeod, how are you getting back to Skye?"

"Well, I'll take the 15:53 bus to Fort William and then another bus to Broadford. It should get me there at nine o'clock this evening."

Liv pondered again.

"Seems like a long journey. Why not spend the night on board *Ravnsvart*? My father is getting out of hospital tomorrow and as soon as I have him aboard, I plan to head for Kyle of Lochalsh. We need to re-fuel there and meet up with Jimmy Ritchie. We could drop you off. I think you'd enjoy the sail."

The Rev jumped at the opportunity.

"I'd love that. Thank you. I'll phone Shona and let her know I'll be a day late. I'll still be in good time for Ewan's funeral on Friday."

That settled, Frances and Richard disembarked from *Ravnsvart* for the last time. Frances started the Renault's engine, engaged gear and with a wave, the pair departed from Oban's North Pier and headed for the A85 and the long haul south. After a stop for refreshments and a stretch of the legs on Loch Lomondside, they reached Dalmannoch just before nine o'clock that evening.

NEW LOVE

WHEN they left Professor Ruairidh Macdonald at his home overlooking Loch Ness almost two weeks before, Frances and Richard had been concerned at their friend's sense of loss and humiliation following the departure of his wife Fiona with his two children. The professor's melancholic state of mind was to persist for the next ten days, until that stormy Saturday when, unbeknown to the professor, those aboard *Ravnsvart* had their dramatic confrontation with *Whiteman Pioneer*.

As it happened, Ruairidh had agreed to be one of the speakers that day at a seminar for Gaelic teachers in Inverness's rather swanky Kingsmills Hotel. The theme was employment available to those who had gone through Gaelic medium education and how to promote these opportunities.

Ruairidh's half hour slot was delivered in the morning just before the lunch break, and over lunch he found himself sitting next to a teacher at one of Inverness's secondary schools. Their conversation was of course in Gaelic, but is translated thus:

"I enjoyed your presentation Professor Macdonald. I don't suppose you remember me. I was one of your students about eight years ago. You were Doctor Macdonald then."

"Yes, certainly I remember you – Mairi – em – Mairi Campbell. What's been doing with you Mairi?"

Mairi explained that, after graduating, she had gone to the Canadian Maritime Provinces of Nova Scotia and Prince Edward Island to teach Gaelic and broaden her horizons. She had recently returned to Scotland to teach in Inverness.

When the afternoon session was over, and the attendees were preparing to depart into the wind and the rain, Mairi sidled up to Ruairidh and asked, "I'd love to hear about what *you* have been up to Professor Macdonald. Would you like to come round to my place for a coffee before you go home? I just live nearby."

"Why not, just for a wee while, but I think we can dispense with the Professor Macdonald. You're not a student now. Ruairidh will be fine."

And so the professor followed his former student's chic Mazda two-seater sports car in his ancient Volvo V70 Estate to her semidetached house in the Drakies area of the town. Over coffee, once ensconced in armchairs in Mairi's cosy home, Ruairidh described his work in Galloway and how he had got involved with the development of Dalmannoch. Mairi, in turn, talked about her youth in her native Isle of Tiree and, as the conversation flowed, so did Ruairidh's attraction to this interesting, intelligent, amusing and self-assured woman. Her shapely figure was set off by a short tartan skirt into which was tucked a close fitting white top that enhanced her well-formed breasts. These attributes, coupled with her soft lilting Tiree Gaelic had a seductive effect on the professor.

The tête-à-tête continued as each discovered more about the other and afternoon passed into evening.

Mairi then suggested, "You'll stay for dinner? I can rustle up some pasta."

Ruairidh thought for a minute of the prospect of being home alone, microwaving a 'ready meal' and

218

replied, "Well if it's not too much trouble; that would be very nice."

So Mairi set the table, prepared the meal, lit candles, dimmed the light and opened a bottle of red Italian wine.

"Ah wine, I can't", the professor protested, "I have to drive home."

Mairi looked out of the window at the ferocious rain squalls and then smiled, a mischievous smile.

"Och, why not just stay over. It's really wild out there. I have a spare room here."

Not unwillingly, Ruairidh agreed.

"Why not indeed, I haven't enjoyed myself so much for – well – for some time."

Over dinner and wine, the conversation became more intimate.

"You know Ruairidh, when I was studying at the institute, I had a bit of a crush on you. Of course I was a mere student and you were an older married man, so – well – unobtainable."

Ruairidh sighed, "I'm flattered that a bonny young girl like you would have thought me attractive, but I'm afraid my star, such as it was, has fallen. My wife walked out on me a month ago. She's gone off with another man."

"Yes I heard. But you know, I have a feeling that your star will rise again soon. You are a handsome and attractive man."

"And you Mairi are a rather naughty, but very attractive woman and you have certainly cheered me up."

Once the meal was over, Ruairidh helped by washing the dishes as Mairi dried them. Mairi reached up to put some glasses in a cupboard. Her skirt hitched up to reveal a shapely thigh and as her breast brushed Ruairidh's cheek, he felt a tingle in his nether regions that he had not felt for some time.

Ruairidh took her hand to steady her. He looked her in the eye and said.

"Thank you for a lovely evening."

Then he kissed her full on the mouth.

Mairi wrapped her arms round him and held his kiss for a long time and then moved her hand slowly down his back to his bottom and pulled him close towards her.

She whispered, "The pleasure's mine and the night is still young."

They kissed and cuddled as Ruairidh's hand cupped and fondled Mairi's breast and each gradually explored the other. At length, Mairi took Ruiridh's hand and pulled him through to her bedroom where they fell onto the double bed. The bed in the spare room lay undisturbed.

*　*　*

From that delightful night onwards, Ruairidh's star *did* rise again. Mairi and he became an item. He often stayed overnight at her semi, which was handy for his MacPhedran Institute of Celtic Studies and, from time to time, she also stayed at his house, *A Cheapach*, with its magnificent Loch Ness views. Mairi was, of course, almost fifteen years younger than Ruairidh, but she had packed in a lot of life experience, not least with men, and she seemed to have a wisdom beyond her years. She found in Ruairidh a stability, comfort and intellect that suited her and, above all, she was physically attracted to him. Mairi, who was, herself, a classy dresser, bucked up Ruairidh's rather staid tweedy dress sense so that he now sported more snappy and colourful attire. All in all Ruairidh felt rejuvenated. The partnership worked.

At first they kept their relationship quiet, but as they were seen together at social events, the theatre or merely out and about, the affair was soon in the open. One major step was the weekend when Mairi was introduced to Ruairidh's twin daughters, Catriona and Eilidh. They had been hit hard by their parent's separation, so there was some apprehension on Mairi's part as to how she would be accepted. In the end the girls, who were very fond of their Dad, were thankfully quite relaxed about his new partner.

Ruairidh found it quite ironic that, while his Macdonald's traditional suspicion of Campbells and their works had been vindicated by Dale Campbell luring his wife away, he had found new love with a lovely Campbell from Tiree.

One interest of Mairi's that Ruairidh was fascinated by was her experience in Nova Scotia, an area to which thousands of Highlanders had emigrated during the infamous Highland Clearances. Mairi had been collecting stories and songs from the still extant, but now greatly depleted, Gaelic community in Canada's Maritime Provinces. This interested Ruairidh greatly. He was well aware of the cultural links between the Highlands and Nova Scotia, but had never visited that part of Canada.

"I'd love to delve into all this a bit more. Maybe we should go to Nova Scotia together and have a good look around. Meantime, I think there may be a good conference in it for Dalmannoch, because there is a

Galloway connection too. The *Lovely Nellie* took emigrants from Galloway to Canada in 1774."

Mairi was excited by Ruairidh's interest in her own area of expertise.

"I'd love to go to Nova Scotia with you Ruairidh. I have a lot of friends there and in P.E.I.[14] But you talk a lot about Dalmannoch and Brother Richard, Frances, Hector and the rest of them. They sound like an interesting bunch. I'd like to go there to see what it's all about."

Ruairidh smiled and put his arm round his new love.

"Well you shall, because I, and 'companion', have been invited to Richard and Frances's wedding and you will come with me."

---

[14] Prince Edward Island

DALMANNOCH DEVELOPMENTS

WITH the return of the travellers, life at Dalmannoch seemed somewhat humdrum after the dangers and excitement of the previous few days. Before returning to Canada, however, Hector stayed on at Dalmannoch for a week, partly to rest and recuperate, partly to visit his relations James and Hilda Douglas at their nearby estate called Glenshillan, and partly to look at the outline design the Dalmannoch Trust's architect, Jamie Arbuckle, had come up with for expanding sleeping accommodation on the site.

Hector and Richard examined the outline drawing that their architect spread out on the table in Dalmannoch's kitchen. The result was a simple well-mannered two story building of traditional design. Six en-suite double bedrooms on each level opened onto verandas that ran the length of the building, giving the whole a rather pleasing colonial look. Jamie proposed locating the accommodation building to the rear of the main Dalmannoch building, so that it formed a courtyard between the two.

Richard responded: "Very interesting Jamie. Extra accommodation for up to 24 people. So with the caravan and three guest rooms in the existing building, not counting your apartment, Hector; that would give us over 30 bed spaces in total. That would generate real income and make a big difference to our ability to market residential courses, and events."

Hector agreed, but, businessman that he was he wanted to get down to the arithmetic.

"Okay, so let's say 12 rooms, plus another four we already have, at 50% occupancy and say £50 per room per night. That's – let me see – about £140,000 per year income. Then there are running costs and servicing a mortgage. What sort of building cost are we talking about Jamie?"

The architect stroked his chin, as architects are wont to do.

"Well, the trust owns the land, so that cuts out a big chunk, but then there's utilities, access road, parking and the furnishings. I think we can do it for under half a million. It's fundamentally a pretty basic structure."

It was Hector's turn to stroke his chin.

"So if we could secure a mortgage for say £400,000, at present low interest rates, we might be talking about £25-30,000 per year for 25 years. It might just work, if we can pull together a hundred k deposit – even if you have underestimated the cost, Jamie, as, in my experience, architects almost always do."

Jamie responded with mock horror, "Oh, ye of little faith!"

There was a short pause as the whole concept was pondered and then Richard chipped in, "But we don't have a £100,000 deposit. We raised forty odd thousand at the festival, which was excellent, but a fair bit of that is already committed. That leaves a big gap."

Hector raised an eyebrow.

"There may be ways and there may be means. I'm sorry I missed the festival, but it has undoubtedly raised the profile of Dalmannoch. I think we could launch a crowdfunding campaign on the back of that. Then, I'll need to check up on things back in Vancouver, but if all's well, maybe I could chip in a bit myself."

Hector turned to Jamie Arbuckle, "What sort of timescale do you think we could be working to?"

"Well, depending on planning and building consents and having funding in place, I'd say about a year, less if we were lucky."

Hector looked at Richard and nodded.

"It looks as though we have a proposition worth pursuing. Let's put some more flesh on the bones, get Duggie to refine the figures a bit and put it to the board for approval?"

Richard readily agreed.

As the three of them examined the drawing further, Hector mused for a couple of minutes.

"It's a strange thing: As you know Richard, the Illuminati, in their evil goal of world domination, set out to create monopolies by destroying my logistics business and Ragnar's tidal energy work. Those were two of their stated objectives. They had a third and, I suppose overriding one, which was to suppress interest rates by manipulating the Federal Reserve, that is to say the central banking system of the United States.

Well, my son-in-law, Brad Linley, and our legal adviser Eustace Blake have been doing some digging and they confirm that for some time the Illuminati have indeed been secretly influencing the Fed. I got a very interesting email from Eustace describing this only yesterday. So in a way, while they were a curse to Ragnar and me, they are a help to the Dalmannoch Trust in keeping the western world's interest rates at rock bottom. I suppose we should be thankful for small mercies."

The Illuminati and the Federal Reserve were subjects of which Jamie Arbuckle knew nothing and while Hector was expounding on these strange matters, Jamie unrolled and laid out another outline drawing on the table.

"This", he declared with a sweep of his hand, "is my concept for a new gathering hall to greatly enhance the trust's ability to host large events in all weathers.

Richard and Hector looked in some wonder at the drawing.

"I have gone for a heptagonal, that is to say, seven sided, plan, so that the exposed roof truss will be in the shape of an Elven Star[15], which will actually be very robust."

"Wow. That's clever. I like it. What do you think Richard?"

"Yes, it looks wonderful, but I shudder to think what it will cost and where we will find the money to build it."

"I guess it's one for the future, Richard, but I'd reckon it's something we could aim for in the longer term."

Hector turned to Jamie: "Would you like to talk us through your thinking?"

"Sure thing. The idea is to create a flexible multi-purpose space for events, conferences, dances, musical or dramatic performances – anything of that kind. So there is a stage more or less opposite the entrance, and a linking structure that joins the hall to the current dining room and kitchen in the existing building with space for a café, toilets and store – all designed to generate income in as efficient and, if I may say so, elegant a manner as possible. You will see that I have specified a turf roof and, with good insulation and solar panels, the whole

---

[15] A seven sided interlaced star, being the emblem of the Wigtown Wicca Coven and the Galloway Knights of Peace, otherwise known as the Elven Knights

thing will be pretty well carbon neutral – in fact it should generate power for the main building."

Richard was impressed. In his youth and later at the Whitleigh Priory where he had been a postulant brother, he had developed a considerable skill in building work and he could see immediately the practicality of the proposal and the boost it could give to the whole Dalmannoch enterprise.

"I think it's magnificent. Maybe one day we will find a way to fund it. Mind you it would have been an ideal venue for our wedding reception next month. However, we will just have to make do with the chapel, dining room and library."

"Make do?" exclaimed Jamie, "The Dalmannoch chapel is one of the most beautiful buildings in south west Scotland."

"True, true; which reminds me, Frances and I are due to lodge the marriage notice with the registrar today in Whithorn. If I'm late Frances will have my guts for garters. I'd better scoot."

WEDDING ARRANGEMENTS

AS always with weddings, even relatively small affairs such as that of Frances and Richard, there was much to organize. Of course, it was the women-folk who were most excited about the whole process of planning and preparation. There were guest lists to assemble, dresses to select, catering to organize, details of the ceremony to decide, who was to take on which roles and of course to make sure all the key requirements of the Church were approved by Father McGuire, for both Brother Richard and Frances, as Catholics, wanted a Nuptial Mass.

All this transpired in the four weeks between the registration and the big event.

Guests from distant parts started to arrive in the few days before the wedding. First of these to appear was Frances's mother, Nuala, who had set off that morning from her home in Letterkenny, County Donegal. Frances and Richard drove over to the port of Cairnryan to meet the ferry from Belfast. This was to be the first time Nuala had been to Dalmannoch and her first meeting with Richard.

With a motherly hug, Nuala McGarrigle's first words were of course with her daughter.

"Oh ma dear, it's so lovely to see you." And then tellingly looking at Frances's tummy, "How're you doing?"

"Just fine Mam. Everything's just fine. I'm so glad you could come over." And then turning to Richard, "And this is my lovely Richard."

Richard smiled and held out his hand.

"I'm very pleased to meet you at last Mrs McGarrigle, and if I may say so, as a Devonian, welcome to Scotland."

"Thank you Richard, it's good at last to see the man that Frances is to marry."

The trio made their way to Frances's Renault. Richard took the wheel and mother and daughter sat in the back seats. On the journey back to Dalmannoch, Frances and her mother understandably had a lot of catching up to do, but Richard felt a coolness towards him on the part of Nuala.

On arrival, Nuala was shown to her room, after which she was given a tour of the building, the chapel and the grounds. She had to admit that, while she had feared that the pair were living in some sort of dilapidated hippy commune, she was, to the contrary, quite impressed by the whole set up and with Richard's quiet enthusiasm and obvious care for Frances.

Over a cup of tea and cake, Nuala McGarrigle confessed, "I have to say that I was disappointed that the pair of you decided to conceive a child before you tied the knot. But I can see, Richard, that you are a kind and caring man and a great improvement on Francie's previous husband"[16]. She added, "And of course you are a Catholic, so my first grandchild will, I hope, be brought up in the Faith." And then to show her approval of the forthcoming union, she produced from a cardboard box a christening gown wrapped in tissue paper.

---

[16] Frances's previous husband, Gerry Flynn, who had been an abusive gambler, was killed in a stand-off with police as described in Dalmannoch - The Affair of Brother Richard, ISBN 978-1-905787-68-5

"I want you to have this Francie. It's an heirloom from the O'Brien side and well over a hundred years old. You and I were christened in it and your grandmother before us."

Next to arrive, of the travellers from distant parts, was Hector Woodrow Douglas, who had picked up none other than a still slightly limping Ragnar Torkelsen at Edinburgh Airport and who was accommodated in the guest bedroom of Hector's Dalmannoch apartment. Of course Hector took a proprietorial pride in taking Ragnar for a tour round Dalmannoch and showing him the plans for the proposed building works.

The arrival of that pair was followed by Professor Ruairidh Alasdair Macdonald and his new love Mairi Campbell. They had arranged to stay, as usual for the professor, at the Steam Packet Inn at nearby Isle of Whithorn. Ruairidh and Mairi soon palled up with Hector and Ragnar and were fascinated and amazed to hear of their adventures of the previous month.

Meanwhile Shona MacLeod had arrived to stay with the Rev and his family and had arranged to hang out for a week or so, which was much to Frances's delight for she had become fond of Shona after the short time she and Richard had spent with her in Broadford.

Then, on the day before the wedding, of those others who had to travel a distance, Richard's Aunt and Uncle, Ann and Aubrey Wells, arrived from Brixham. They were also billeted at the Steam Packet Inn, partly because the little port of "The Isle" had some resemblance to the kind of Devon harbour with which they were familiar. These relations were quickly followed by Frances's brother Finbarr and his long-standing live-in girlfriend Imelda from Dublin. They were accommodated in another of Dalmannoch's bedrooms.

The final distant arrival was Dom John Ainsley, Prior of Whitleigh Priory by the pretty Cotswold village of Wethercott St Giles, where Richard had been a postulant monk. Richard was honoured that the prior had agreed to say a concelebrated mass with Father McGuire and, of course, arrangements had been made for the prior to be a guest of the father at St Aidan's parochial house.

Meanwhile, that afternoon before the wedding, in secret, Suzie Silver, Holly Garden and some of the other women from the Wigtown Wicca Coven set to decorating the chapel with exotic flowers that had been obtained by special arrangement from the Logan Botanical Garden. The display exhibited some discreet Pagan symbolism that would be un-noticed by any but themselves. It was, however, otherwise agreed that, out of respect for the sacred Catholic sensibilities of the much loved main participants, the Wicca group would play down their own adherences.

As per tradition, it was considered unlucky for the groom to see the bride on the night before the wedding, so Richard was sent to the Steam Packet Inn where he was to spend the night at the same location of his aunt and uncle, Mairi and Ruairidh Macdonald who was to be his best man. He was delighted to catch up with the news of Brixham from his Uncle Aubrey and Aunt Ann. They were equally delighted to see how their foster son had grown in confidence since his troubled youth.

The company at the Steam Packet Inn swelled when Hector, Ragnar, Whisky and Holly joined them for a couple of hours and there was much reminiscing over recent events and escapades that Ruairidh, Hector, Holly and he had had previously. Old Aubrey and Ann could hardly believe that their quiet Richard could have had such adventures since they had last seen him.

In the course of their rambling chat, Ragnar mentioned that Hector had shown him the plans for a new Dalmannoch accommodation building and the seemingly unaffordable heptagonal hall. Ragnar then added:

"Hector tells me that, now that his business has stabilized after the attack from Whiteman Inc., he is going to fund the outstanding balance for the accommodation building. I think that is good – very good. Well, I am here, like him and the rest of you to celebrate the marriage of Richard and Frances. I do have another reason. It is this. Richard, Frances, Hector, Holly and Whisky came to help me defeat an evil and deadly foe. Without that help we could not have won through, and I would have been ruined and probably killed. I can't thank them enough. I know they are each committed to the development and financial stability of Dalmannoch. My business too has stabilized. What I would like to do, is pay the full cost of erecting and furnishing the – what is it called? – the heptagonal hall."

There was a stunned silence and then Richard exclaimed, "Ragnar Torkelsen! I can't believe it, Are you sure? It's going to cost a packet."

Ragnar smiled, "Richard, I'm a wealthy man, I've been relieved of a great burden, thanks to you and your friends. The cost is not a problem and it would be my pleasure."

Richard shook the big Norwegian's hand, lost for further words.

Back at Dalmannoch that evening, the women-folk had been doing their thing. Dresses were tried on and final details such as favours checked and double checked. The three tier cake, which had been baked and iced by Suzie Silver, was produced and admired, then things settled down over drinks and nibbles whereby reassurances were offered to Frances about the morn's big day.

Frances was only too glad, after all they had been through, since they had first met a year and a half before, that she was to spend her, hopefully quieter, future with the man she loved and the child she was soon to bear.

WEDDING BELLS

THANKFULLY, for a mid-November Saturday morning, the weather was settled, cloudy and relatively mild for the time of year. Of the three maids of honour, Suzie and Holly arrived early. Imelda, Frances's quazi-sister-in-law, who was already staying in Dalmannoch, slept in, tired after her journey the previous day and suffering from a hangover from the previous night's conviviality, was last to appear.

"Oh b'Jaezus, I overdid it a bit last night with the booze."

After breakfast and strong coffee, Imelda rallied round with the others and the three maids of honour set to their duties, in their rather sexy green satin A-line knee-length dresses, representing fertility. Clearly fertility was already proven in Frances's case, but it was felt that the concept should not be ignored. The maids of honour fussed round Frances to make sure that she looked her best for her nuptials. Of course Frances's mother acted as a kind of overseer of the operation, offering advice, welcome and otherwise.

Although now six months pregnant, Frances looked stunning in her ivory dress with crossover neckline, knee-length skirt and silk satin ivory sash. The whole ensemble was set off by a lace capelet and completed by an orchid in Frances's dark hair.

As she stood in front of her daughter in admiration, Nuala had a tear in her eye, a tear of happiness, motherly pride and a little sadness.

"Oh ma baby, you look so beautiful. It's just a pity you Da' didn't live to see this day."

She gave Frances a big hug.

Frances returned the embrace warmly, but protested, "Mind me hair now, I don't want Richard to think he's marrying a trollop."

The wedding ceremony was scheduled to start at eleven o'clock. As the venue was next door in the chapel, there was no need for a car. Twenty minutes before commencement, Hector Woodrow Douglas, Chieftain of the Green Douglases, appeared, resplendent in full highland dress, with plaid and two eagle feathers in his bonnet. He would act as substitute father of the bride.

Frances gasped, "Oh, Hector, you look magnificent. What an honour".

"On the contrary, Frances, the honour is mine, to have such a beautiful woman on my arm."

After this mutual admiration, Nuala, Finbarr and the maids of honour headed to the chapel. Nuala and Finbarr were ushered to their places at the front on the left by Dalmannoch's kilted treasurer and secretary, Duggie Gordon, while the maids of honour stood at the back to await the arrival of the bride.

Meanwhile Richard, his best man, Ruairidh, and his aunt and uncle had taken their places at the front on the right, while the other guests, who were mostly mutual friends of bride and groom spread themselves where they could, filling the chapel.

There was quite a buzz until Ann Morrison, on the organ, struck up Jesu, Joy of Man's Desiring, and all stood as three altar boys from St Aidan's entered the nave with cross and candles. They were followed by Prior John Ainsley and Father Tom McGuire, both in their finest vestments, as they processed to the altar.

They took their places and Ann struck up Pachelbel's Canon in D which was the sign for a radiant

Frances to enter on the arm of Hector. They proceeded down the aisle, followed by the smiling three maids of honour. Once they reached the altar, Richard moved to stand beside Frances, while Hector sat beside Nuala with the maids of honour sitting behind. Frances looked at Richard and saw him as she had never seen him before, in a well cut dark suit, with shiny black shoes, white shirt and silk tie. She liked what she saw. Eying Frances in her wedding dress, Richard realized that he loved this Irish woman more than he could express.

After a few words of welcome from Father McGuire, the Mass continued with a hymn and readings and a short homily. Then at last came the moment for which everyone had been waiting. Prior John Ainsley moved towards the couple for the sacrament of marriage. He asked:

"Richard and Frances, you have come here to enter into Marriage without coercion, freely and wholeheartedly?"

Richard and Frances said together, "I have."

"Are you prepared, as you follow the path of Marriage, to love and honour each other for as long as you both shall live?"

Richard and Frances together – "I am."

"Are you prepared to accept children lovingly from God and to bring them up according to the law of Christ and his Church?"

Richard and Frances together – "I am."

Prior John continued: "Since it is your intention to enter into the covenant of Holy Matrimony, join your right hands, and declare your consent before God and his Church.

"I, Richard Wells, take you, Frances, to be my wife. I promise to be true to you in good times and in bad, in sickness and in health. I will love you and honour you all the days of my life."

"I, Frances McGarrigle, take you, Richard, to be my husband. I promise to be faithful to you in good times and in bad, in sickness and in health, to love you and to honour you all the days of my life."

Prior John, acknowledging that the couple had declared their consent to be married, declared, "Whom God has joined together, let no one put asunder. I now pronounce you man and wife."

Rings were placed by each on the other's finger and Prior John blessed the couple.

"You may now kiss the bride."

An audible sigh went round the chapel and many a happy tear was shed.

The remainder of the Mass need not be detailed here, but in view of recent adventures, among the hymns sung was the sailor's hymn, 'For Those in Peril on the Sea'.

Richard and Frances duly signed the register, witnessed by Ruairidh and Holly, and after the nuptial blessing Ann pulled out all the stops and blasted out Wagners's Hochzeitsmarsch, which was the signal for bride and groom to process down the aisle and out of the chapel, followed by the best man and maids of honour, Nuala and Hector, Ann and Aubrey and the rest of the guests.

Outside, the clouds had parted, the sun shone and there stood the Reverend Donald Angus MacLeod, his pipes rending the midday air with 'Mairi's Wedding'. Once all had exited the chapel, groups were arranged for photographs, after which everyone repaired to the main Dalmannoch building for the reception.

A year and a half before, Dalmannoch had been in a moribund and shabby state, until Brother Richard had been given the task of sprucing it up and finding a new future for the building. That he and his fellow travellers were successful in this and much more, was demonstrated by a fully restored, tastefully decorated and functioning enterprise. Its one drawback in hosting a wedding meal was that, despite its recent expansion, the dining room was not really big enough to handle the numbers attracted to Frances and Richard's nuptials comfortably. Nevertheless, somehow, everyone managed to squeeze in.

Cocktails and canapés in the common room preceded the sit-down wedding breakfast – a grand affair provided by outside caterer friends of Suzie Silver. Then came the speeches. Ruairidh, as best man, was in good form, having got over his melancholy following separation from Fiona, and finding a new love in Mairi Campbell. Ruairidh's renewed confidence showed in the wicked humour of his address.

After the speeches, the newlyweds made the first cut of Suzie's cake, which was then sliced and distributed as the desert course, after which came the party which spilled over into the common room. The ceilidh music was naturally provided by the Galloway Gaelic Group, whose lively talents had been honed to perfection by practicing for the festival. To kickstart proceedings, Richard and Frances led the first dance to The Pride of Erin Waltz. Hector then took Nuala on to the floor to be followed by others. In no time the place was rocking with the Gay Gordons, Canadian barn dance, strip the willow, another waltz, and so on.

By the late afternoon, when the party was in full swing and dusk was falling, Richard and Frances, now changed into smart casual clothes, said their farewells and made for the trusty Renault Magane. The whole crowd came out to cheer them and shower them with confetti as they got into the car, which had, of course, been decorated with 'JUST MARRIED' sprayed on the back window and ribbons tied to the door handles. As the newlyweds drove off to a clatter of trailing tins, it is perhaps appropriate to give Ragnar the last word.

"They are a fine-looking couple of good character. May Fate give them a long and happy life together."

EPILOGUE

WITH the return of Richard and Frances from their short honeymoon and as life at Dalmannoch settled into something resembling normality, it may be wondered what became of those evil monopolistic forces that had been motivated by the Illuminati to do such harm to the enterprises of Hector and Ragnar.

Harry Hunter and Reg Pemberton were of course merely pawns in a much bigger game. Harry was found guilty of attempted murder. Charges of piracy and terrorism were dropped, partly on the grounds that he had been acting under threat of death and partly as he had been co-operative in giving evidence that pointed the finger of guilt for the murder of Councillor MacLeod and Lachie Mackinnon at Reg Pemberton. Harry was given a ten year sentence.

Reg Pemberton was soon tracked down, charged with and found guilty of their murder. He got life for his pains.

The adverse publicity brought about by these court cases and the enquiry into the loss of *Whiteman Pioneer*, together with other revelations of corruption stateside, caused the collapse of Whitelite Power and the near insolvency of the parent company Whiteman Inc., which had to withdraw from the Canada-China trade. In the course of these events, Woodrow Douglas Logistics were awarded $6 million damages against Whiteman Inc.

As a consequence, Hector's company was free to prosper and Ragnar Torkelsen was able to pick up several of the Whitelite licenses, which strengthened his hand in developing his tidal stream energy projects. Ragnar had found a new friend in Hector and a mutual interest in supporting the Dalmannoch Trust. With both their financial inputs, construction of the new accommodation block and heptagonal hall was soon under way. In recognition of their generous support, Dalmannoch Trust decided that these new buildings would be called The Woodrow Douglas Building and Torkelsen Hall.

Of the Illuminati, its members continued in their quest for world domination, but their wings had been seriously clipped and their influence was greatly diminished.

Then in mid-February, Frances gave birth to a bonny baby girl. She was christened Nuala Ann in the O'Brian christening robe in Dalmannoch's wonderful chapel.

And so,
a new beginning